MOVING IN FOR THE KILL...

Slocum stung *El Comandante* with two long jabs. He stepped in again, jabbing him once more, then hooked him hard in the mouth, drawing blood.

El Comandante had not been hit like that in ages—and never by a *prisionero*. His convicts all knew the consequences of provoking his wrath—the torture chamber, the flogging post, the sweatbox, the endless weeks on starvation rations. It was easier to climb in the ring and passively accept their thrashing.

Slocum hooked him again, and a terrified hush settled over the crowd.

No, this Slocum was no ordinary convict. Fighting him would be an entirely new experience. He wiped his mouth with his black leather gloves, smearing them with his blood, and the salt sweat stung his cut lips.

El Comandante decided he liked the sensation . . .

JAKE LOGAN

SLOCUM BUSTS OUT

BERKLEY BOOKS, NEW YORK

SLOCUM BUSTS OUT

A Berkley Book / published by arrangement with
the author

PRINTING HISTORY
Berkley edition / September 1990

ISBN: 0-425-12270-0

A BERKLEY BOOK® TM 757,375
Berkley Books are published by The Berkley Publishing Group,
200 Madison Avenue, New York, New York 10016.
The name "BERKLEY" and the "B" logo
are trademarks belonging to Berkley Publishing Corporation.

PRINTED IN THE UNITED STATES OF AMERICA

10 9 8 7 6 5 4 3 2 1

To Joe Crockford
Who's always been there

Special thanks to
George Schneider
For his help and encouragement

And to
The late Eddie Witzel
Time-when and for-all-tomorrows

Scratches don't count,
In Texas down by the Rio Grande....

—Frank Desprez, "Lasca"

Part 1

A promise made is a debt unpaid,
And the trail has its own stern code. . . .

—Robert W. Service

1

The two men squatting by the mountain stream wore dirty *peón* clothes of white muslin. The shorter one carried a haversack containing miner's tools, a carbide lamp, and blasting powder. The older one, the tall dark gringo with the long flowing mustache, was shaking his head.

"I ain't goin' back down," he said. "This mountain's snakebit, I tell you. It's killed our blaster and timberman. It's almost killed you and me."

"*Amigo*, we can do it."

The gringo continued to shake his head. "Never happen. This be a government claim we're jumpin', and Díaz, he ain't wastin' no time. He's got six *federales* lookin' for us already. They cut our sign, it's gonna be two more for the sycamore. Time to *hasta mañana* out of here."

His *mejicano* friend had a hawk nose, dark brown skin, and eyes black as chips of coal. While he brooded on Slocum's advice, his eyes became even darker.

"But the vein, *amigo*, you saw her? She is *magnífica!*"

"We're out of shorin' timber, and what's hammered in's cracked and comin' down. As for the air, there ain't none—just dust and gas. I tell you that pit's a hell hole."

"I will do the digging. Shore up the tunnel after me. It is all I ask. One more week, one more day, and I will dig

3

more gold for you than you will spend in a lifetime. In two lifetimes.''

"Rodriguez is dead under a ton of rock. Buenavista got burnt up in the fire. When we dug out Otero''—Slocum shuddered at the thought—''he was et whole by rats. I ain't followin' suit.''

"Please, *amigo*.''

"You go down that hole, I'm pullin' stakes—leavin' you to rot. You ain't got both feet in the stirrups no more. You hear me, boy?''

"Amigo, por favor.''

"Get your stash. It's time to slope on outa here.'' The big gringo stood. "I'm closin' up that hole.''

Slocum headed down the mountain toward their base camp.

2

Slocum had struck camp and packed both animals when he heard the muted rumble of the underground explosion.

Roberto had gone back into the mine.

Slocum had a mind to dig up the stash, load it onto the jack, and leave Roberto down there to die.

No way he was returning to the pit.

No way at all.

Far as he was concerned, Roberto was dead.

3

With gritted teeth Slocum lowered himself into the shaft. As he payed out the pull-rope, the windlass creaked and the ore skip beneath his feet lurched and swayed.

Finally, Slocum reached two-shaft, where Roberto had found the main lode.

Tying off the cable, Slocum entered the tunnel. Less than three feet high, it was supported by a dense maze of shoring timber. Bending over, trying not to bang his helmet on an overhead beam, he started into the tunnel to check on his friend.

Every inch of the shaft seemed booby-trapped. Sharp fragments of rock jutted out of the walls and ceiling, and the floor was littered with deadfall. Slocum felt as if he were picking his way through a forest of knives.

The number one crosscut, then the two, then the three.

He was making less than twenty feet an hour, and his face and body were ripped by the protruding rock. The shoring timber groaned and coughed incessantly, and he was running out of air.

At the fourth crosscut—where he was to turn toward Roberto's main stope—his worst suspicions were confirmed. The last ten feet had collapsed, and his partner was on the other side.

He went to work clearing out the deadfall and hammering in the broken shoring timbers.

4

Halfway through the cut, he heard Roberto call to him.

"*Ey, amigo*, I knew you would come back for me."

Slocum paused. Mines are never quiet places, even during the best of times. The timbers groan and crack under the weight of their "hanging rock." The tunnels ring with the din of deadfall and reverberate with the shrieking of rats. Dust pockets explode. Shafts collapse. Men curse and scream and die.

Now the mine seemed quiet.

He did not take it as a good sign.

"That's right, *amigo*. I came back."

"You shall be glad you did."

"Yeah, I'm thrilled already," Slocum said, digging.

"You will be more thrilled when you see the gold. Ey, we are lucky today. We shall be so rich. Nuggets b-e-e-g as your *garrocha*. It was indeed the mother lode."

"It'd help if you did some diggin' 'stead of jackin' off your jaw."

"I am a l-e-e-tle cramped for that. But it shall not take long. And trust me, you will be well paid. The gold, she is *fan-tás-ti-co*. And she is all for you."

"We was supposed to split even—fifty-fifty."

8

"*Sí*, but this gold is special. I make it to you as a gift. For your friendship. *Por favor*."

"*Por-fuckin'-favor*," Slocum mumbled to himself as he continued to clear the deadfall and prop up the collapsing shaft.

5

Four feet and four hours later, Slocum broke through. In the dim glow of his carbide lamp, he found Roberto pinned at the waist under a ton of rock.

That he was alive at all Slocum found incomprehensible.

Roberto managed a grin. "This is my lucky day, no?"

He pushed a grain sack toward Slocum.

Slocum emptied the contents. A dozen jagged rocks, dirty and misshapen, but the real thing.

Slocum hefted them. They were big as his fists—maybe sixty pounds in all. Slocum figured they assay out at 80 percent—as much gold as the rest of them had mined in a year.

"It was never the gold, *amigo*, you knew that."

Slocum nodded. He did know it.

"All the years in these mines," Roberto said, "even in the hell mines of Sierra Magdaléna, I dreamed of such a find. *Cuál es?* What is it you gringos call it?"

"The mother lode."

"*Es verdad.*" That is right. "The lode of our mothers. I could not leave this mountain without seeing her, touching her, possessing her."

"Sounds like she's possessed *you*," Slocum said.

"*Es verdad*. She is no lady at all but a *puta*." A whore.

10

"No real lady'd send us down here," Slocum agreed.

Slocum hefted one of the nuggets. Even in the dim light of his carbide lamp, it glittered.

"Let me get this other load off you," Slocum said, pointing at the rock pile pinning his legs and midsection to the tunnel floor. "Then we can haul ass out of here."

"Do not lie, *amigo*. You lie to a dying man, you go to hell, no? You came back for me, and that is enough, *muy bueno*. You do not have to lie."

"I can't leave you, Roberto."

"*Por favor*. This shaft, she is not so safe."

"Never happen."

Roberto grinned. "Then this is my lucky day, to have such a fine friend, one who will not leave me here, to die in the dark and the dust, alone."

"Too many rats."

Roberto stopped grinning. It was true. He could hear them even now. The smell of his blood was driving them mad. Roberto could hear them scrambling and shrieking, worming their way through the drifts and shafts.

Toward him.

"The timber," Roberto said, "ain't gonna hold no more, and the mountain, she will come down on you too. If you wait, you die. So go, *amigo*. *Vaya con Dios y diablo*." Go with God and the devil. "While you got time."

Slocum did not know if he could do it. Four years of war followed by thirteen more on the owlhoot had cost him pretty near everything—much more than he could afford to lose. He had no casual friends. He'd lost so many at places like Shiloh and Cold Harbor, at Manassas and Bloody Lawrence, that he'd come to see them as luxury he could no longer afford.

Friends were something he'd taught himself to live without.

Still Roberto was different. They'd gone through so much together in these pits—so much sweat and blood, violence and death. Somewhere along the way Roberto had cracked Slocum's shell, gotten through to him. Slocum couldn't help himself. He and the Mexican were not only partners, he liked him. That was the hard-tail truth. He liked him.

Roberto was his friend.

Roberto was a man. There was no doubt about it. More guts than you could hang on forty miles of line fence, he never walked away from a fight, never backed down from a cold bluff, and never drew out on a friend. You knew who he was, what his word was worth, the things that count.

You could ride the river with him.

"I'm sorry I drag you down here," Roberto said.

Slocum shrugged. "You heard me bitch?"

"No, but I hear the rats. They come quick now. I tell you, you must go."

"You be still. I got to get to them rocks. I gotta get you out."

Of course, it was a lie. The rats *were* closing in, and his friend was pinned down too tight. He would die in the dust and the dark, no matter what Slocum said. There was nothing he could do.

Nothing.

With his left hand, he wearily closed Roberto's eyes.

He tried to think of words, but did not know what to say.

Words had never been his long suit.

"I got no complaints," he finally said.

With his right hand, he cut Roberto's throat.

He held his head while the body settled.

Then it came to Slocum—his issue of big-time trouble. He heard it first as a faint grumble, a low growl. The rumbling was soon followed by bursts of black dust billowing down the shaft. Then the rumble accelerated—like the distant roar of a locomotive—till it was one protracted, hair-raising howl, the crazed baying of killer wolves.

Now the roar was elemental, and Slocum's world was breaking up. The timbers, invisible under the smoky black dust, buckled and screamed, lurched and cracked, writhed and collapsed.

How long Slocum was unconscious he could not say. All he knew was that when he came to, he was lying there, almost asphyxiated by the cave-in, half blinded by the inky dust.

He could not even turn around to dig his way out.

He was going to have to dig his way into the stope, find an old cut, a drift, a manway, some tunnel somewhere that would get him out of this pit.

Jesus God, he was in for it this time.

He tied Roberto's bag of rocks to his belt and started to dig. In the background he could hear the rats.

Part 2

Wars breed crime and criminals; and the American Civil War did not differ from others in this respect. Out of the dislocations of that conflict grew a wave of lawlessness that transcended all expectations in the length of time it lasted, and in the number of successive generations in which it perpetuated itself.

—Paul L. Wellman,
A Dynasty of Western Outlaws

6

Night in the canyonlands.

Two men in linen dusters stood guard at opposite ends of the canyon. The rest of their group—six men and one woman—hovered around the campfire. They sipped Arbuckles coffee and Old Crow bourbon.

The firelight glittered brilliantly up and down the pass. Eerie shadows of the men, woman, and their horses flickered on the canyon walls, and the heat cut through the night chill.

They listened to the desert—to the droning locusts and to the whistling swoop of the bullbats. A nearby pack of coyotes yelped and barked, and on the rimrock a puma screamed. In the distance an owl hooted. The Apaches believed its piercing cry portended death, and while the tall man in a brown sweat-stained plainsman's hat wasn't so sure, he touched the dirty buckskin amulet strung from his neck nonetheless. This smelly pouch was filled with feather moss, garlic, and mustard root and was believed by many to be a charm against evil. Frank James wasn't any more convinced of its protective power than he was of the owl's ill will.

Still he continued to finger the charm.

17

7

It was near midnight when Frank approached his younger brother. The man was off by himself, down-canyon, wrapped in his horse blanket, reading the *Police Gazette*. Its cover purported to "Protect the Public Morality by Exposing the Bawdy and Bloody Conduct of That Legendary Outlaw Lady, Belle Starr, the Bandit Queen!" Above that promise was an illustration of a dark-haired cowgirl slinging a blazing six-gun, a snakewhip cracking in her other hand.

"Amusin'?" Frank asked.

Jesse James lowered the magazine. He grinned, and his gold-crowned upper molars gleamed.

"Ain't found nothin' this amusin' nohow—not since Lincoln got his gruel from John Booth."

"Well, I'm glad someone's cheerful. I'm startin' to think I should've hit church on Sunday."

"That's a fact," Jesse said. "We all ought to keep the Sabbath."

"Yeah? Well, what I want to know is, how did you end up with this crowbait? When you wired me in Texas, you said you had 'a merry band to rival the Youngers.'"

"I exaggerated. They just don't make studs like them Youngers no more."

"These boys couldn't whip the Youngers' sisters," Frank said.

"They're not that bad."

"Not that bad? When them Tucson deps are putting holes in you big enough for a blind man to piss through, when the hot air's whistling through them jagged wounds and the buzzards are breakfastin' on your eyeballs—and this gutter trash, this pack of spittoon swampers, is yellow-tailing it out of town—I want to hear you tell me how they ain't *that bad.*"

"I still say they ain't that bad."

Frank James looked apoplectic.

"Bob Ford's with us," Jesse said. "Hell, he was with us at Blue Cut when we robbed the Glendale train. Tom Planck and Dick Bane, you remember them from when we sacked Lawrence."

"I remember them as two-bit egg-suckin' peckerwoods."

"I know you ain't had time to get acquainted with the Lopez brothers, but—"

"You mean them *madre*-pimping *hideputas* you must've scraped off some clap-stinking whorehouse wall."

"Goddamn it, Frank, they ain't that bad. Neither is Belle."

Jesse sneaked the last part in fast.

"That tears it. Bringing a low life whore on a job proves you've jumped the rails. Belle-Goddamned-Starr? Cole Younger couldn't control her when they were married, and she was only eighteen. What do you expect you can do with her now?"

"Frank, she comes with the job."

"Why?"

"She's the one what cased the bank."

"So?"

"I give her my word."

"What do you care?"

"It's my word, ain't it?"

"It's ain't your word what counts, little brother. It's *who* you give it to."

From up the canyon Frank heard a whistling *hiss,* a *crack,* and a *clink-clink, clink-clink, clink-clink.* As the woman entered the glow of Jesse's fire, Frank saw she was swinging a wrist quirt with a leaded stock and two heavy lashes of plaited rawhide with three-inch poppers on the ends. Dressed in faded Levi's, black blouse, and Stetson, she slapped the *cuarta* across her knee-high riding boots heeled with six-inch buzz-saw rowels. Loose chains clanked behind the heels, and janglers clinked inside the rowels.

Her Levi's were so tight they looked ready to burst. She wore a black gun belt and a holstered Navy Colt. She wore the top three buttons of her black work shirt boldly open and carried a saddlebag slung over her shoulder. Her Stetson was canted at a rakish angle. Under the tilted brim, Frank caught a glimpse of the slanting black eyes, wayward, filled with wickedness.

Still cracking the quirt against one bootleg, Belle stared at Frank. "You sure don't think much of these boys."

Frank snorted.

"He says they ain't exactly the Younger brothers," Jesse answered.

"Nor Shelby nor Bloody Bill nor Quantrill neither," Belle agreed.

"But they'll do," Jess said.

"Do for what?" Frank asked. "Chicken stealing? Cleaning privies?"

"They'll do for that Tucson bank," Belle said.

Jess put down his *Gazette* and stood. At five feet eight he was two inches shorter than his brother.

"Anyway, I feel lucky," Jess said.

That brought a derisive snort from Frank. "If it weren't for bad luck, you wouldn't have no luck at all."

Another man approached them from up-canyon. As he entered their firelight, Frank saw it was Bob Ford. Medium height, with ginger hair, the young man was wearing a black slouch hat and a steel gray duster. He was wearing the nickle-plated S&W .44 Jess had given him. He was grinning.

"Woo-ee," Bob Ford yelled. "Jess, we gonna get it done tomorrow. Them good old folks of Tucson ain't never gonna forget you. You're going to have another governor cursing your ass besides Crittenden back in Missouri."

"Wonder why old Crittenden hates me so," Jess said.

"You seem to forget that letter you sent him," Bob Ford said. "You threatened to cut his heart up in strips and eat it."

"You watch that highsidin', boy," Frank said to his brother. "This ain't Missouri, and Yuma Prison's a hell-hole."

Jess shook his head. "Never happen. They ain't putting me in no cage—not like they did them Youngers. Heeled and hidied 'em to a barn door. Ain't nobody doin' me like that."

"Not after Northfield," Belle agreed.

"Next lawman throws down on me," Jess said, "I'm holding court in the street."

"Amen to that," said Frank.

"I heard you once robbed a parson's poor box," Bob Ford said to Jess.

"At the time I was conducting his boys' choir."

"You're a hard man, Jesse James," said Belle.

"More sinned against than sinning."

"Tell that to that Pinkerton agent, John Whicher," Frank said. "You sent him to hell."

Jess reached into his own saddlebag, down by his blanket, and plucked out a newspaper clipping.

"Here's a real desperado," Jess said. "This Charles Guiteau—he shot President Garfield, and every time the prosecutors try to get a word in edgewise, he jumps up and cuts them off. The other day he shouted at the prosecutor: 'It is the unanimous opinion of the American people that you are a consummate jackass.' Says here he yelled at one of the witnesses: 'Is there no end to this diarrhea?' "

"Yeah," Frank said dryly, "he's a real smart man. When's he due to hang?"

Belle snorted, then reached into her saddlebag and took out a bottle. Popping the cork, she read the label aloud.

"Lydia Pinkham's Vegetable Compound: *The Positive Cure for All Female Complaints*. That be the case, I best take some right now."

The three men looked at her, skeptical.

"That stuff work?" Bob Ford asked.

"You bet it does, put enough tincture of opium in it." She helped herself to a healthy swig.

Frank James shuddered.

"Zzzzzzzzzzzzzzzzz."

Over by the canyon's talus slope, they heard the racheting buzz of a diamondback. Bob Ford drew his .44.

"Don't worry," Jess said. "I trapped them in a grain sack. Thought I might save them for breakfast."

"What?" Bob Ford was incredulous.

Jesse shrugged. "Diamondbacks ain't as meaty as I like, but if you fry them up in oil and garlic, they're mighty good eatin'."

"You gonna eat them snakes?" Bob Ford asked.

"I'll eat at least one. Gonna save the other for that bank

president, in case he don't open up that safe the way I tell him to.''

''Now that's an idea,'' Frank said. ''I got to admit. That's an idea.''

8

Frank James trudged up-canyon to his bedroll. Dawn would come in less than four hours, and he was already tired—tired to his soul. With infinite weariness, he lay down.

But before he could shut his eyes, Belle was kneeling over him.

"You meant what you said earlier?" she asked, helping herself to another swig of her opium-laced snake oil. "Callin' the gang here crowbait and gutter trash."

"Truth is the old gang weren't much better."

"Coleman Younger wasn't no gutter trash," Belle said firmly. "Neither was Jim and Bob."

"Our cousins, the Youngers, excepted," Frank said sleepily.

"Jess says you're just moody. Says you never wanted in on this job in the first place."

"I got land in Clay and Jackson counties. Raised me some prime beef, and Annie's winning prizes for the hogs. Any luck, Crittenden'll be defeated, and I'll get me a pardon. I'll be able to live out my life a free man, under my own name. I'll get off the owlhoot."

"You don't think Jess will?"

"I seen Jess work as a machinist, a millwright, a cowhand. I seen him try to plow fields with three pistols stuffed in his belt. I seen him try a lot of things, and he never got none of them right—not if it was legal.''

''Then why'd you come?''

''To talk him out of it. To talk him into comin' back to Jackson County.''

''You don't like the job? The way it's laid out?''

''I don't like anything 'bout this job. I don't like anything's been *near* this job.''

''But I laid it out good. We can 'scape to Mexico, and I cased the bank myself. Hell, it ain't even no proper bank, not really. It's a cheese box, a tobacco can. We'll take that bank the way Lee took Manassas.''

''Which the Yankees got now.''

''That don't mean nothing.''

Frank gave Belle a hard stare. ''This ain't Missouri. These ain't our people, and *we* don't know the land. As for the crowbait Jess's signed up, I'd as soon be ridin' with Red Legs.'' [Union guerrilla forces in the Missouri Civil War]

''Why you comin' along?''

''Jess needs me.''

''That all?''

'' 'If it be a sin to covet honor, I am the most offending soul alive.' ''

''What's that mean?''

''Literature. You wouldn't understand.''

''You and Jess do go on, what with your books and things.''

''Speaking of Jess, he be needin' you about now.''

''You want me to do you first?''

Frank gave her a slow, off-center smile. ''You turned soiled dove on us, Belle?''

''No better'n I was meant to be.''

''Like your daughter, Pearl?''

''Can't help it if she turned Daughter of Joy. Done the

best I could with her after Cole run off. Whupped her to a frazzle. She just wouldn't mind.''

"Like some I know."

"That be the truth."

"You best do for Jess."

"Sure I couldn't interest you?"

"I ain't got the gumption. If I doused Annie, she'd fix me proper.''

It was Belle's turn to grin. "So marriage turned you mountain oyster?"

"But not Jess. He's your bantam cock tonight."

"That he be, sport. That he be."

9

It didn't take Belle long to get back to Jesse. He was forty yards south of the main camp, sitting on his saddle blanket, his head against his McClellan. He was once again reading his *Police Gazette* by candlelight. Belle sat down beside him.

"What do you think of them good ole boys yonder?" she asked, pointing to the main camp.

"I think there's a wolf in Grandma's bed and a worm in every apple."

"And Satan's wearing a Santa suit?"

He put down his magazine and gave her an appreciative nod.

"Don't let them get behind you, Jess. Keep them in sight."

"You mean tomorrow?"

"Crittenden's got a fifty-thousand-dollar reward out on you. Them good ole boys ain't forgot that."

"I know."

"That's cash money, not some bank job might send us all to Yuma."

"Or propped up on a cooling board," Jess said.

"Hell, with the re-ward. Them Lopez brothers would kill you for your boots. For the heels."

"What do you think of Bob Ford? Frank says he worships the water I walk on."

"A little boy with a big hat. The boots wear him."

"Damn, Belle, you need some more of that Lydia Pinkham."

Belle picked up his *Police Gazette*. " 'For Those Painful Complaints So Common to Our Best Female Population,' " she read from an advertisement.

"Especially when you doctor it with opium," Jess said. His grin was infectious.

"I swear, Jess, one day your smiling optimism will get us all killed."

"Or rich."

"Or both."

He plucked the *Gazette* from her hands and leaned back against his McClellan. In the cloudless purity of the desert sky, the Milky Way was a broad swath of white light, the stars glittered, and the moon blazed. By the light of his candle, he could actually read.

"Still can't sleep?" Belle asked.

"Never could."

She scooted up beside him. He was still reading the piece on "Belle Starr, the Bandit Queen." The *Police Gazette* promised "for the sake of public decency to reveal each of her evil and obscene deeds in lewdly lascivious detail."

"Must be exciting," she said.

"Yeah, this Belle Starr lady sounds like hot stuff."

"You believe everything you read?"

"I believe nothing I hear and half of what I see."

"Then why bother with them dime dreadfuls? Why not try the real thing?"

She jerked the magazine from his hands and grabbed his crotch.

"Whoa, girl. I'm a married man. I don't swing no wide loop."

"You say the same thing every night."

"I just want you to know that Jesse Woodson James ain't no cunt-struck cowboy."

"I know. He's a principled man," Belle said, turning toward him.

As she pressed her face against his, it seemed to him as if her mouth were the hottest thing he had ever felt.

Still he was honor-bound to make one last protest.

"And I say you're the Whore of Babylon."

Belle looked up at him, her eyes glinting with wickedness.

"If you can't stand the heights," she said, "don't climb the mountain."

"Please," he whimpered, "my heart can't stand the action."

"Then keep hell hot for me, you sissy sonofabitch."

With dismaying precision she unbuttoned his fly.

10

In Frank James's nightmare it is always the same. He is in Northfield, Minnesota, slouched at his table at J. G. Jeft's restaurant. As he studies the First National Bank across the street, he lets his bacon and eggs grow cold.

Down the street, Jess, Bob Younger, and Charly Pitts, in linen dusters, trot their thoroughbreds across the iron bridge spanning the Cannon River. They dismount in front of the bank and enter.

Cole Younger and Clell Miller ride up Division from the other direction. They too dismount, pretending to adjust their cinches.

Through the bank window Frank can see Jess ear back the hammer on his .44 and vault the teller's counter. Bob and Charly brandish their pistols and manhandle the cashiers.

Clell Miller stands guard outside the bank, his hand inside his linen duster.

Then everything goes wrong.

People up and down the street are screaming: "Robbery! Get your guns! The James brothers are robbing the bank!" Suddenly, every roof has a shotgun, and every window a repeating rifle. Gunfire pours down on the street.

Cole Younger and Clell Miller jump onto their bucking,

crow-hopping horses, throwing lead in every direction.

Frank leaves the restaurant and heads for the bank. Through its open window he can see Jess pistol-whipping the cashier, shouting:

"Open that safe or I'll blow your head off!"

The dandified cashier, dressed in a white shirt and eye-shades, protests:

"I can't. It's time-locked."

Charly Pitts slits the man's throat.

"We're getting shot to pieces," Frank shouts to Jess, and waves him out of the bank.

He swings onto his horse. More riflemen fire from the roofs and windows. Businessmen take to the streets with Colts. Laborers armed with scythes and rakes block off the streets with upended wagons. Schoolboys chuck bottles and rocks. Little girls, swinging from the bell ropes, ring the church bells. The river steam whistles wail and scream.

Frank can still see the slaughter.

—Clell Miller knocked off his horse with a load of buckshot to the face, then shot through the chest as he struggles to remount.

—Bill Chadwell shot through the chest and dragged by his horse.

—Jim Younger's jaw blown off.

—Cole Younger hit in the side, shoulder, leg.

—Bob Younger shot in the right knee.

—Frank himself hit in the thigh, blood filling his boot.

As they flee the town, Cole goes back to save his brother Bob.

At this point Frank begins to scream.

11

Dawn in the canyonlands.

Frank found himself drenched in sweat, a cocked gun in his fist, being shaken awake by Jess and Belle.

"Damn, Frank, that was a bad one."

Bob Ford walked up in his long johns, also armed.

"It were the worst yet," Ford said.

Jess waved the others away.

"You're strung too tight, Frank," Belle said. "Should've let me do you like I offered."

Frank shook his head.

"Naw," Jess said, "he's too upright for that. Too much hard-bone rectitude."

"Frank prefers his nightmares."

"Calls them 'death-dreams,'" Jess said.

"Has a bad conscience," said Belle.

"You holed as many men as Frank, you'd sleep hard too."

"I holed my share."

"What you want?" Frank asked, glaring at the two of them. "Some kind of medal?"

"We could all use some medals," Jess said. "All that fightin' we done in the war, we never got no decorations. Quantrill didn't believe in decorations."

"Nor in uniforms," Frank said.

"He believed in money, whiskey, and the black flag," said Jess.

"No quarter given," Frank said.

"And in women," Belle said. "He believed real good in us ladies."

"And in fast horses," said Jess.

"Just like Cole," Belle said. "Hated to use a horse hard or a woman easy."

"You sure you don't want to skip this bank?" Frank asked.

"We got to do it," Jess said.

"Why?"

"'Cause it's there."

"That ain't no reason."

Jesse swept his arm across the horizon toward Tucson. "I feel right now like Alexander the Great. 'When Alexander saw the breadth of his domain, he wept, for there were no more worlds to conquer.' That's how I feel. Except we're fortunate. We got one more world. That Tucson bank."

"And after that?" Frank asked.

"We back off."

"You mean that?"

"Sure as shit stinks and buzzards eat carrion."

"Buzzards don't eat carrion," Belle pointed out. "Vultures do."

"Same thing."

"After Tucson we back off?" Frank asked.

"No more banks."

"Nor trains."

"Gospel?"

"Straight tongue."

It was Belle's turn to snort. "The day you two give up

the owlhoot, the ducks in Missouri'll start wearing slickers and rubber boots.''

"Might take up the Word this time," Jess said, giving Belle and Frank each a serious stare.

"Jess," Belle said, "you look at me that way I feel like somebody just stepped on my grave, like I'm eyeball deep in hell.''

"You serious?'' Frank asked Jess.

"Righteous. You and me'll both take up the cloth. We'll pack them in for miles. Imagine it: the James brothers preachin' the Word to the sinful. We could use our own wicked lives as our text. We'd make more money than Morgan, Carnegie, and John D."

"We could head back to Jackson County," Frank said. "We could start now."

"Never happen."

"Why not?"

"We got one more bank to rob.''

12

Bob Ford squatted by the breakfast cookfire. He was pouring himself a cup of coffee from the fire-blackened pot when Tom Planck and Dick Bane approached. The Lopez brothers were close behind. Lawson, Noches, Zapata, and the half-breed they called One-Eye were still passed out drunk under a nearby saguaro.

The two gringos were outfitted like himself—in standard trail garb. Dirty collarless shirts, faded Levi's, and sweat-stained Stetsons. The Lopez brothers dressed *charro*-style in short jackets, white muslin shirts, black pants tapered tightly around the thighs and tucked into their boots. The one they called Cholo wore a straw sombrero with a steeple crown and a three-foot brim, while his brother favored one of embroidered gray felt, heavy with trail dust. Their guns were holstered butts forward, and across their chests were strapped crisscrossed bandoliers, the loops filled with shiny brass cartridges.

Planck carried a bottle of trade whiskey, which he offered to Bob Ford. Ford shook his head.

"We wanted to sound you out," Planck said, his voice already thick with drink.

Ford shrugged.

"We heard them Jameses not only rob banks and trains,"

Dick Bane said, "they hold out on their partners."

Dick Bane moved up beside Ford.

"You was at the Blue Cut job," Bane said. "You see your end?"

He hadn't but wrote it off as blood under the bridge. He figured to do better this time.

"I was satisfied," he said.

"That's bullshit," Planck said, then belched. "You boys come up short."

"Heard it from Jim Cummins," Bane said.

"You figure to call out them Jameses," Ford said, "you best be holdin' something in your hand 'sides snakehead whiskey and empty words."

"I no care who they is, *amigo*," Emilio Lopez said. "My brother and me, we get our share."

"And we're gonna settle it *now*," Dick Bane said, slapping his holstered Colt.

"I'd walk soft," Bob Ford said.

"Like you done at Blue Cut?" Planck said.

"There be six of us and two of them," Bane said.

"Not countin' their whore-lady," Planck said.

"You think to hold the handles on them two," Bob Ford said, "think again."

"They're just *dos hombres, amigos*," Cholo said. "They die like us all."

"And they bleed *también*," Emilio said.

"Fine," Bob Ford said. "Just remember that—when the wind is whistlin' through your eyeballs and the vultures is pullin' your intestines out your ass."

"Just talk, *amigo*," Cholo said.

"I'll compliment your *mamacita*," Ford said, "on your *machismo*."

"I'll take them brothers on right now," Planck said.

"This ain't no speech, friend," Bob Ford said. "This is

right down there in the dirt.'' He threw his coffee in the fire. ''You call them out, they'll break your bones for marrow.''

''We ain't afraid,'' Emilio said.

''You're drawin' blind,'' Bob Ford said.

''But you know different?'' Planck said.

''I peeped their hole card, and I'm here to tell you, it's redder'n blood and blacker'n the grave.''

''You talk about them two,'' Planck said, ''like they's some sort of devil's spawn—fiends from hell that's cloaked themselves in human flesh.''

''I'm givin' it to you straight tongue, pistols on the table. Them two's plagues, locusts, lightning bolts—more trouble than Jehovah gave the Jews.''

''We ain't letting this slide,'' Planck said.

''What do you want on your gravestone?'' Bob Ford asked. '' 'In the Fullness of his Youth' or 'Shot Dead'?''

''I just want my cut,'' Bane said.

''Let it be,'' Ford said.

''What's that supposed to mean?'' Planck asked.

Ford hocked and spat. ''You're mouth's writin' checks your ass can't cash.''

13

Jesse James squatted before a tarnished metal mirror propped up on his saddle. He was attempting to shave.

This was no easy matter. The Great Sonoran Desert was the devil's own frying pan, and today's temperatures would soar above 118 degrees with zero percent humidity. Already the air was so parched the soapsuds dried before he could put a razor to them.

He braced himself for a dry shave.

Out of the corner of his eye, he noticed Belle button up her shirt.

"Hey, girl," Jess said, "don't you ever wash up?"

"It ain't Saturday."

Jess shook his head and began dragging the cutthroat razor over his dried-up lather. Belle got up and walked over to him. He was stripped to the waist, and she paused to study his physique.

"You'd have a fine body, Jess, if it weren't for all them scars and such."

She had a point. Even in the tarnished metal mirror, his history was plain. Two bullet holes—red as slaughter—in his chest, several more in his thighs and groin. Further down, there was also that fractured ankle, which had mended badly and still gave him pain. A Yankee rifle ball had shot off part of a finger.

Belle was standing behind him now.

"How's Frank doin'?" he asked.

Frank was sitting on his bedroll, a dozen yards up-canyon, his head in his hands.

"He says we're cursed by God."

"God ain't been smilin' on us lately."

"Not after Northfield."

"I think He be partial to hard work and sweat."

"He don't seem too fond of our partners neither."

"They ain't got much bottom," Jess said.

Frank joined them. "Thinner'n cow piss on a flat rock."

"Give 'em a chance," Jess said. "They'll grow on you."

Frank chawed his plug a moment then spat. "You can't shine shit."

"Suppose things get rough," Belle asked.

"They'll run for it," Frank said.

"I think they'll stand up," Jess said evenly.

"You know they was real successful rustlers when Jess and me found them," Belle explained.

"Pigs or chickens?" Frank asked.

Jess finished shaving. He wiped the razor on his pant leg, then turned to face his brother.

"What's the matter, Frank? You afraid they'll sell us out? Tell them marshals we *made* them rob that bank?"

"They'd tell 'em Jesus ran a whorehouse if it'd save them from Yuma."

"You really think they'll run for it," Belle asked, "if things get tight?"

Frank took aim at the bag of diamondbacks, then splattered it with tobacco juice. The bag exploded with hissing and buzzing.

Frank stared at his brother. "Like lizards off a hot rock."

14

Belle was pouring one last cup of coffee when she saw the rest of the gang coming toward them. She put down the pot and walked over to their pack mule. She began smoothing out the pack pads.

By the time the boys reached Jess, she was swinging the crossbucks onto the jenny's broad back.

Jess was still squatting by the fire, drinking coffee. Frank stood off to the side, chewing tobacco.

"Jess," Planck said, "there's a couple of things we got to settle."

"Damn straight," Bane said.

As if for emphasis, the Lopez brothers spread out around the the cookfire.

Belle started stacking gear between the sawbucks.

Jess stared at Planck.

"Don't just stand there," Jess finally said, "chokin' on your spit, say something."

"We ain't talked how we're gonna divide up the loot," Bane said. "We got to get that settled."

"Frank and me already decided that," Jess said.

"You ain't said how that's gonna be," Planck said.

"You'll know when we tell you."

"That ain't gonna do," Planck said. "It just ain't good enough."

"We figured to split it even," Bane said.

Bane helped himself to a large swig of whiskey, then belched. Planck took the bottle from him. He upended it next and did not stop till he was sucking air.

"I'd say you boys got a drinkin' problem," Jess said.

"They're hollow to the heels," said Belle.

"Must be," Jess said. "Drinkin' like that before a job."

"Listenin' to your brother scream nights's what done it," Planck said.

"Makes a man wonder," said Bane, "whether Frank here's got what it takes. Whether he's worth an even split."

"Makes a man wonder," said Planck, "whether it ain't time to move on, find another game."

Now Emilio was upending a mescal bottle.

"Better go easy on the hooch, boys," Jess said softly. "We got a bank to rob."

"Not till we settle on what our end's gonna be," Bane said.

"I'm decidin' that," Jess said.

"The same way you decided it at Blue Cut?" Planck asked. "I hear you settled your partners right out of their split."

"It wasn't me said nuthin'," Bob Ford said. "They heard it from Jim Cummins."

"Don't matter where we heared it," Bane said. "We ain't trustin' you two with nuthin'."

"Jess," Planck said, "I wouldn't trust you to carry a dozen eggs across the street."

"Cholo?" Jess asked. "Emilio?"

"*Sí, amigo,*" Cholo said.

"*También,*" said Emilio.

The Lopez brothers fanned out four more feet, forming

a semicircle around the Jameses. Cholo stopped just in front of Belle's pack mule.

"See, *amigo,* I no care who said what. I no care you cheat your *compadres. Ey,* I say *mucho bueno, por favor!* A compliment on your *machismo!"* He lifted his mescal bottle and took a long pull. "I say I like you, *amigo.* I wanna be jus' like you. I don't wanna pay you neither. Or your brother. Or your *puta."*

Belle looked up from her packs. She didn't like the odds. Jess was standing there in boots, black pants, and a white collarless shirt. He had a Smith & Wesson .44 in a half-breed shoulder rig and a Navy Colt strapped to his hip. Frank was still stripped to the waist and weaponless.

If Jess made a play, they'd die where they stood.

"Bob," Jess said, "You takin' sides?"

"Deal me out on this one," Bob Ford said.

"Belle," Jess said, "you got any opinions?"

"Whores ain't got no opinions," Planck said.

"They just got pussies instead," Dick Bane said.

"Since I ain't got no opinions," Belle said, "maybe I'll just finish packin' this ani-mule."

Belle hauled on the lash rope. The kyacks, panniers, and crossed wooden sawbucks creaked and groaned, till the load pulled together. She threw the diamond hitch and tied it off. The mule lunged sideways, blew a long rolling snort, and shied bites at Belle's shoulder.

"I'm better with jacks," she said.

"Frank?" Jess asked.

"It's your play, little brother."

Cholo's eyes glittered crazily. "You wanna do it, *amigo?* You wanna get it done?"

"You can always crawl," Bane said.

"Yeah," Planck said, "and afterward Cholo here'll do you like a girl."

"That'd be somethin'," Bane said, glancing back at Ford, "watchin' your hero get heifer-branded by a spick."

"Aw, hell," Jess said. He grinned at Belle so widely his gold-crowned back molars gleamed. "Goddamn it to hell."

His hand flashed for the .44 in the half-breed, while Frank was reaching for the slip-hammered Colt shoved in his belt behind his back.

Cholo's Remington had already cleared his holster.

Belle had the stagged-off hand-grip Greener out from under the crossbucks. The six-gauge scattergun was no more than ten inches long, from its chopped-down stock to its sawed-off double-barreled tip. She aimed it elbows locked, arms extended.

The camp rocked with the Greener's roar and filled with a blinding cloud of black-powder smoke. Cholo was blown face-first into the cookfire.

The second hammer click was audible, even above the ringing in their ears.

"Belle's first barrel," Jess said, "was loaded with cayenne pepper and birdshot. The other's lye and number two goose if you want a taste."

"Belle," Frank said, "it was Planck there called you a whore."

"I think she's a real lady," Planck said.

"Same here," said Bane. He glanced at Cholo and looked like he was going to be sick.

"He was your brother, Emilio," Jess said. "You lookin' for satisfaction, I'll accommodate you."

Emilio kicked his brother out of the fire. Cholo's mescal bottle was still in his fist, miraculously intact. Emilio picked it up.

"How much *dinero* you say in the-e-e-s bank?"

"Ninety thousand gringo dollars."

Emilio pulled the cork out with his teeth and spat it at

his brother's scorched head. He took a deep swallow and handed it to Jess. Jesse joined him in a drink.

"Ninety thousand gold simoleons cuts a lot of family ties," Bob Ford said.

He helped himself to the bottle, then handed it to Planck.

Bane had to yank it out of Planck's mouth to get some. Bane took a deep pull and tossed it to Belle.

She caught it one-handed, the other still holding the Greener. Her trigger finger never wavered. She took a drink.

She stared at Emilio. "It's one more share for all of us, *compadre*." She handed him back his brother's bottle, which he finished.

"You want to bury your brother?" Frank James asked.

"The-e-e-s bank," Emilio said, "it e-e-s a long way, no?"

"Nine miles," Jesse said.

Emilio turned toward his horse. As he stepped over his brother, he dropped the empty bottle on him.

Frank threw an arm over the Mexican's shoulder. "Emilio, you're a *muy macho hombre duro*."

"I could learn to love you in the daylight," Belle said.

"Damn straight," Jess agreed. "You're my kind of man."

15

The James Gang stopped on a hill a quarter of a mile outside of Tucson.

"Any bright ideas?" Frank asked his brother.

"Same as before," Jess said. "We ride in, rob the bank, and ride out."

"Not quite," Belle said. "We do this one with a little more finesse."

"Finesse?" Jess was dubious.

"Yes," Belle said. "Frank, Jess, and me ride in first. Give the place a look-see. The rest of you ride in in groups of two and three. Take your time. Try to look natural."

"Okay by me," Frank said. He looked at Jess. "Okay?"

Jess nodded.

Emilio belched.

Frank stared at Emilio, hard. The man was very drunk.

"You sure you want in?" Frank asked.

Emilio was working on a new mescal bottle.

"My brother let himself get killed by a *puta*. I piss on his grave. *Me cago en su puta madre.* I piss in the milk of his mother."

"That's your *mamacita* too you're pissing on," Belle reminded him.

"I piss on her twice."

"He don't share your exalted view of motherhood," Jess said to Belle.

"Our *mamacita* was stinking *puta*." Whore. "I piss on her three times." He helped himself to another drink.

"What do you know about the marshal?" Frank asked Belle.

"J. P. Powers? He's a hardcase," Belle said. "An ex–Red Leg and an army major."

"He crosses my sights," Tom Planck said, "he'll be a dead major."

"How much firepower we lookin' at?" Frank asked.

"Just him and three deps," Belle grinned. "Like I said, he's a hardcase, but the town council don't let no townfolk carry guns. They keep all the firearms boxed and tagged over at the jail. So this won't be like Northfield. Get past Powers and his deps we're home free."

"Lawson? One-Eye? Noches? Zapata?" Jess asked, checking on the four sick drunks. "You men sit a horse?"

They were not much good, but they were still on their mounts.

Lawson nodded.

Noches managed to mumble a *"Sí."*

One-Eye shrugged.

Zapata grunted, *"Quizás."* Maybe.

"I'll take that as yes," Jess said.

"Bob Ford," Frank said, "you're stayin' with the remuda, here on this hill."

"I'd rather be with you at the bank."

"Don't be givin' us no complaints," Jess said. "We need a good man to guard these mounts."

"We get a posse on our trail," Frank said, "horses'll be worth more'n the damn gold."

"That's a fact," Jess said.

"Guess were ready," Belle said.

"Guess we are," Jess agreed.

"Then let's get it done," Bane said.

"Yeah," said Jess, "let's get it done. 'Fore Emilio starts pissin' on his mama again."

Part 3

A man must never count himself lucky——
until he is dead.

—Aeschylus

16

John Slocum was at peace. Leaning back against the brass headboard, he reached over to his bedside bottle, tossed back another slug of Jackson's Sour Mash, then lit his fourth Havana of the day.

He paused to caress the long flame red hair of the naked doxy, presently going down on him. She was doing an extraordinary job. He was glad he'd hired her for the week.

The Excelsior Hotel in Tucson was a far cry from the claustrophobic shafts of the pit. In the light of an overhead scroll-pattern crystal chandelier, Slocum stared not at collapsing shoring timbers and black exploding dust pockets but at the triptych mirrors of an exquisite Louis Quinze cherrywood dresser. In its three mirrors, Slocum gazed not on the grisly prospect of bloody death but on his massive brass bed with its fringed spread of red satin, the heavy mahogany drawing table with its narrow high-backed armchairs, the hearth-blackened fireplace with the handsome reproduction of Turner's *Slave Ship* above the mantel. On the teak bedside table in a silver-plated bowl floated a bouquet of white and yellow desert blossoms.

And beside the bowl was, of course, his bottle.

Nor was there a rat pack attacking his privates. The woman presently performing that task was simply the most beautiful woman in Tucson—Doc Holliday's own whore, Kate Elder—and the most expensive hooker the Light of Love Parlor House had to offer.

Yes, he'd never had one like Kate Elder before. Her lips wandered and wondered and whispered the length of his member, assiduously puzzling out macabre mysteries and coy conundrums therein. She murmured honeyed words and half-sobbed sighs. She challenged it to greater heights, greater glory, and darker passions.

The Havana still clenched in his teeth, Slocum tossed back another slug of sour mash. Yes, he was truly content. Sunlight flooded through his open balcony window—another welcome reminder that he was no longer trapped in the hell-pit. No, indeed. His was now a world of shining luminosity, not cramped blackness.

Slocum was free and very much alive.

And very, very rich.

17

Slocum was about to send Kate down for another bottle when a passkey opened the room door.

His fingers closed over the ivory-handled Navy Colt under his pillow, just as Sheriff J. P. Powers filled the doorway.

"Don't pay me no nevermind," Powers said. "What you do in here is your affair. I'm just curious 'bout that eighty thousand dollars you deposited in the First National."

Powers was an older man—close to sixty, Slocum guessed—with iron gray hair and matching gunfighter's mustache. His face, browned by wind and desert sun, was cut with deep lines. He had wide shoulders, narrow hips, and the flat ass of a horseman. He favored a black plainsman's hat, matching coat and vest, and wore his Colts butts out.

Slocum had known a few hardcases in his day. Hickok, Quantrill, Bloody Bill. He'd ridden with the Jameses and Coleman Younger. Powers had been cut by the same stamp.

"Don't see that that's any of your business," Slocum said.

"If I poked around, I could probably scare up some dodgers on you. Can't tell me you ain't wanted *no* place. Either way, you wouldn't like our jail much. It ain't got whores like the Light of Love."

Slocum gave Powers a long look. He'd traveled some hard and dusty trails since the war. He'd been shot nine times and stabbed twice. He'd broiled under the hot sun of Yuma Prison and half froze in a January blizzard eight thousand feet above sea level in the Rockies. He'd met all kinds of men and buried his share. Some had been friends. One or two had died when by all rights it should have been Slocum's turn.

When, after the war, he'd returned home, he found two Yankee carpetbaggers in possession of Slocum's Stand. It was a fair fight. Nobody for counties around said it wasn't. He'd killed the carpetbaggers in the town square of Antrim, Georgia, and had given them every chance.

So after four long years—fighting for a lost cause under a defeated flag—he'd lost everything.

Friends, family, home, all.

He never forgot, and he never forgave.

It was true what Powers said about those dodgers. From time to time Slocum had helped himself to a bank or train, and by his own count had now spent thirteen years on the owlhoot. At least three states and one territory had money on his head, and he had ample reason to dislike any man who carried a badge.

To his surprise, he liked Powers.

"You got some hard bark on you," Slocum said, "bracin' a man while he's at his pleasure."

"Find he's more reasonable with his boots off."

"Wants to answer your questions and get back to re-lax-a-tion?"

"If he ain't got nothing to hide." Powers gave him a faint smile.

"I partnered up with three miners down near Magdalena. The mine was a hellhole and buried all three. You can dig for the bodies, but they're under a mountain of rock."

"But the mountain didn't get you?"

"I was more scared'n them."

"Gonna be here long?"

"Could be. I heard you marshaled for Parker, fought the Apaches, and ran a tight town. Heard the gold might be safe here awhile."

"Might be." Powers's stare wrung him loose then let him go. He reached for Slocum's holstered Colt, hanging from the headboard. "Course we do have an ordinance against civilians bearing arms. But since you're a law-abiding citizen, you won't mind me keepin' this for you at the jail."

Slocum shrugged. He did not tell him about the slip-hammered Navy Colt under his pillow. Or the disassembled Sharps he carried in the traveling case.

"I'm a man of peace," Slocum said, putting his arm around Kate Elder.

"Aren't we all?"

Tipping his hat to Kate, Powers let himself out.

After locking the door, Slocum turned to the whore.

"Now where were we, honey?"

She took up where she had left off.

Slocum, meanwhile, helped himself to another Havana, following up with a generous slug of sour mash.

Almost as an after-thought, he slipped his Navy Colt out from under the pillow and checked his loads.

Part 4

Jesse James killed many a man,
And robbed the Glendale train.
He robbed from the rich and gave to the poor
He had a hand and a heart and a brain.

—Billy Gashade,
    "The Ballad of Jesse James"

18

When the gang reached the outskirts of Tucson, it was midday. Brown adobe shacks baked in the heat, and the few observable *peones* had already begun their afternoon siestas in the shade of their hovels and jacals. A handful of *peone* women in black *rebozos* were still up and around. Each of them had a baby on her hip or slung across her back. The only women who weren't on their feet knelt— grinding corn on flat stone *metates* with hand stones called *manos*.

Otherwise this dusty desert town—surrounded by black mountain peaks and crimson canyons—was deep in its siesta.

As they entered the town, the shacks gave way to real houses with second floors, whitewashed shingles, and verandas. Merchants too had set up shop, and all around her, Belle saw their stores and wares and signs.

TAILORING—LATEST STYLES.

WASHING TAKEN IN.

GROCERIES, HARDWARE, SIGNS PAINTED.

UNDERTAKING—NEWEST METHODS.

They turned onto Main Street. The midday sun was scorching, and except for a lone muleteer wrestling his long-bodied wagon off to the side, the dusty thoroughfare was empty.

Even so, Belle drew her Greener out of its saddle sheath. Her thumb wasn't on the hammer, but it covered her side of the street.

Suddenly a newsboy jumped off the sidewalk. The young boy waved a paper at them.

"Extra! Extra! Wyatt Earp guns down his brother's killer in the Tucson railyards. Read all about it. Want to buy a paper, ma'am?"

"Anything about them hellacious James brothers?" Belle asked.

"No ma'am, but there's lots about Wyatt Earp and Doc Holliday."

"Wyatt Earp?" Frank grimaced.

"That carpetbaggin' Yankee scum?" Belle said. "Too bad."

"Here, son," Jesse James said. He pulled out his poke. Carson City Liberty Heads, double eagles, cartwheels, and big 'dobe dollars. He tossed him a shiny new cartwheel.

"Gee, mister, I can't change that. The paper's only two bits."

"Buy your ma a present."

"You must be an awful rich man," the boy said.

"It's my hope and dream," Jess said.

Jess stuffed the newspaper in his saddlebag, and they continued on. Now there were storefronts and signs everywhere. ROOM & BOARD signs abounded, and the word SALOON was omnipresent. THE BULL'S PIZZLE sign loomed above an obvious watering hole with a painting of a black snorting bull decorating the outside of the second-floor cribs. Across the street were THE EARTHQUAKE SALOON and THE FOUR ACES. Up the block lay THE PALACE OF MIRRORS.

Further up the street Belle could see the word SALOON at least fourteen more times.

At the next corner they passed a sprawling three-story building, covered with white clapboard and gingerbread trim. The yard offered two clumps of shade trees, and the front porch, which was full of swings and gliders, featured a high roof supported by white Corinthian columns. The big upstairs rooms opened onto black iron balconys, and from the second floor a signpost jutted over the sidewalk. Its swinging sign advertised:

LIGHT OF LOVE
PARLOR HOUSE

No ordinary house of ill repute, this was clearly where Tucson's elite took their pleasure.

By now the street bristled with signs. A tawdry two-story building advertized itself as:

DRY GOODS & CLOTHING
Boots & Shoes, Hats & Caps

A smaller shop offered:

Patricia Overbay, Proprietress
DRESSMAKING
Cutting and Fitting
All latest styles

The shop next door stated in bold letters:

Emil Jacobson, Proprietor
APOTHECARY, DOCTOR'S OFFICE & MORTUARY

Featuring Dr. John Bull's Vegetable Worm Destroyer, Hostetter's Celebrated Stomach Bitters, Ayer's Cathartic Pills, Herbal Nostrums, Balm of Childhood, Cuticura Anti-Pain Plaster & Lydia Pinkham's Miracle Tonic for All Female Complaints. Plus All Forms of Surgery and Embalming

"Hey, Belle," Jess grinned, pointing at the sign, "we can get you some Lydia Pinkham's."

"For your female complaints," Frank said.

Belle winced.

"After Lydia turns you into a lady," Jess said, "we can take you next door and fit you for a dress. Ain't never seen you in no dress."

"Must be a sight," Frank said.

Belle snorted.

They passed saloon after saloon—THE FARO QUEEN, THE RED DOG, THE TIN PALACE.

Another small whitewashed shop advertised FRUITS & COLD DRINKS, while a place across the street called itself:

THE CENTENNIAL BARBERSHOP
Dogram & Shenly, Proprietors
Shaving, Shampooing & Baths
Haircutting Done in Latest Fashion

They passed J. C. WICKER'S SADDLERY SHOP. In the window was the most beautiful saddle Belle had ever seen. Black burnished leather, inlaid with turquoise and silver, a matching bridle hung over the horn.

Jess caught the look in her eye. "Think Belle wants to rob a saddle shop instead of the First Tucson National."

Now they approached the town square. There, amid scattered saguaros and clumps of cottonwoods, were the Southern Pacific rail station, a corral–livery stable, and the Hatch & Hodges stage depot.

Across from the train station was a sprawling, four-story building. On its gray shingles was painted:

J. C. Abernathy, Proprietor
GENERAL MERCHANDISE
Firearms and Ammunition
Guns and Pistols Repaired
Agent for the Celebrated Sharps Rifle
Also Ballards Improved Rifle
Also Herculite Blasting and Stump Powder
Pitch and Tar a Specialty
Agent for Charter Oak Stoves
Leavenworth Scientific Stove
Stetson Hats in All Latest Styles and Colors
Agent for the Unrivaled Studebaker Wagon
DEALERS IN EVERYTHING!

"Too much damn greed 'round here," Belle said.

"Yes," Jess said, "greed's a terrible thing to see."

"Maybe we can deliver them from its wicked temptations," Frank said.

It was a lazy afternoon, and only a half-dozen saddle horses were tied up in front of Abernathy's General Merchandise Store.

They swung down and tied their mounts at the hitchrack. Belle paused to study Abernathy's.

"Says they got blasting powder and guns," she said.

"And the sheriff's confiscated the townfolk's guns," Jess said.

"Reckon this won't be like Northfield," Belle said.

"Reckon it won't," Jess said.

They entered the double doors. Abernathy's was big as a barn and packed to the rafters with merchandise. Near the door were the comestibles. Barrels of spices, coffee beans, flour, crackers, beans, and salt pork; huge jars of dried and pickled fruits, candies; kegs of Virginia tobacco and cigars—long nines, supers, stogies, even Havanas—plug tobacco and cable twist, Lone Jack pipe tobacco, and the cowhands' favorite, Bull Durham.

Tables were everywhere, piled high with merchandise of every description—dishes, pots, and pans; fancy soaps such as Sapolio, Pears, White Rose, and Fairy; colognes, hair tonics, razors, and liniments; sundries such as candles, pens, ink vials, and pencils.

The ranch equipment was near the store's middle. Wagon jacks, whippletrees, buckets and pails, harness bells and snakewhips, ox yokes and coal oil lamps, hanging from ceiling ropes and beams.

Many of the tables were now laden with men's clothing, much of it Civil War surplus. Kossuth hats with flat raw-edged brims and high crowns, forage caps, piles of pants and Levi's, broadcloth and gingham shirts, planter's hats, Stetsons, bowlers, and plainsman's hats, slickers and *sarapes*.

Toward the store's center the tables of clothing gave way to equipment and gear. War surplus pommel bags, canteens, haversacks, light sabers, rawhide lariats.

Ropes were strung across the room, and from them were hung carved leather belts and hatbands, coiled lass ropes, quirts of stitched rawhide with leaded stocks and plaited bands, poppers attached to the tips.

Toward the rear of the store a dozen saddles were slung over sawhorses. Three-quarter Montana kacks, Mexican and Texas rigs, Slick Forks, Rim-fires, Bugle Forks, McClellans, and Mother Hubbards, several with fancy skirts and leathers. Over the pommels were hung a variety of bridles—horsehair, rawhide, one- and two-ear hackamores, mecates and romals, Texas reins and thick latigos.

Off to the side were the women's clothes. Belle was more interested in the glass-encased firearms to the rear of the store, but Jess steered her toward the women's fashions.

From ceiling ropes hung floor-length, high-waisted dresses with long sleeves, high necks, and paletots; basque jackets and sacques, balmoral skirts and chemises, petticoats and camisoles.

On the nearby tables was a wide assortment of fancy hats and bonnets, kid-and-cloth shoes, garters, hairpins, curling irons, and bustles.

"Can't hardly picture it," Belle said, shaking her head.

She dragged the Jameses toward the back of the store. Here, the walls were lined with barrels of tar, pitch, grease, coal oil; spools of barbwire; kegs of Herculite Stump and Blasting Powder. Above the barrels and kegs were rifle and shotgun racks and above them shelves were stacked with handguns and boxes of ammunition.

Clearly, the town's gun laws prohibited possession, not sales.

The glass cases in front of them displayed dozens of pistols, including Remingtons and Smith & Wessons, some early Paterson Colts, a pair of big Walkers, the .44 Army model, converted to metal cartridges, and the new Colt .45 Peacemaker. In a separate case was a selection of "Stingy Guns"—four- and six-shot Sharps Pepperboxes, double-barreled .41-caliber Remington derringers with both hook and saw handles. Beside them was an assortment of hide out rigs including a wrist holster.

"The Whore's Revenge," Jess said, indicating his disdain for the miniature weapons.

"You used to carry one in your hat," Frank reminded him.

Jess nodded, grudgingly, then turned to examine the

Walker Colts. A store clerk approached them.

"I'm Otis Foster. Can I help you?"

A tall round-faced man with a bland smile, he was dressed in dark pants, a white shirt with a celluloid collar, and a red bow tie. His brown hair was slicked straight back.

Belle made him out to be a dude.

"Maybe," she said, raking him up and down with a hard stare. "You know something about guns?"

"It's my specialty."

Jesse clapped him on the back and smiled. "Now that you mention it, we *are* on the scout for some firearms."

"From your dusters, I would make you out to be stockmen."

"Market hunters," Frank said.

"Well, since you're looking at pistols," Otis said, "perhaps you need some personal protection. We have some mean mountain lions around here."

"Matter of fact, I was thinkin' of them Walker Colts," Jess said.

"Most powerful handgun made," Otis said, removing the pair from the case. He sighted down the barrel. "Stop any painter alive dead in his tracks." He laid them out on an adjoining oak counter. "Fifteen and a half inches long with a nine-inch barrel, they weigh five pounds each, loaded."

"Sure they got enough stoppin' power?" Belle asked Jess sarcastically

"I'd carry a Gatling," Jess said, "but it stretches my holster."

"Could get to be a problem with the Walker," Otis said. "It's not really meant to be slung on the hip, but on a horse. It's what Colonel Colt calls 'a horse pistol.' Try some of these." Reaching under the counter, he placed a pair of heavy-duty saddle holsters beside the guns. "Let your horse do the hard work."

"Let's look at some rifles," Frank said.

They moved down the counter. Along the wall were a half-dozen rifle racks.

"Pretty near everything a market hunter could ask for," Otis said, pointing to the various rifles as he walked. "Here's a classic Henry repeater. B. Tyler Henry developed it during the war. Forty-four caliber, brass frame, lever action, fifteen-shot rim fire, loads through a tubular magazine under the barrel. Same as the Winchester seventy-three, except some of the new rifles also take forty-four–forty ammunition, same as the new Colts."

"Ain't interested," Frank said.

"Maybe I could interest you in the Old Reliable—the fifty-caliber Sharps. Has the longest effective range of any rifle made. The Apache say, 'It shoots today, kills tomorrow.' A seven-hundred-grain bullet backed by a hundred seventy grains of powder, it'll drop a charging bull dead in his tracks. You interested in market game, you can't do any better."

"I was thinkin' of the Spencer," Frank said.

"My personal favorite," Otis said, taking one down from the rack. "You can carry as many ammunition tubes as you want and reload it in a flash—seven new rounds per tube. And its killing range is up to six-hundred yards, twice as far as the Winchester."

"A new Spencer, a dozen tubes," Frank said, "and one thousand rounds."

"Shotguns?" Otis asked, indicating a wide array of double-barreled scatterguns.

"Any six-gauge ammunition?" Belle asked.

Otis reached under the counter and produced a box. "The owner's personal supply. Has it hand-loaded, special."

"Six boxes," Belle said.

"Know how to shoot them things?" a voice said behind them.

The man was a good six feet two . He had a hard face, salt and pepper hair, and a matching mustache. He was not smiling. Belle had the feeling he never smiled.

The man wore a tan broadcloth shirt with brass cavalry buttons and red suspenders. His black pants were tucked into horseman's boots. He wore a tan stockman's hat, and a nickel-plated ivory-handled Colt was strapped to his hip. A deputy sheriff's badge was pinned to his shirt.

Belle gave him an ingratiating smile. "Naw, but we're willing to learn."

"John J. Hardin's our manager as well as deputy sheriff," Otis said. "There's an ordinance against you firing these weapons inside the town limits, but if you want Mr. Hardin to test them for you out back he will."

Jess turned to Hardin. "You know how to shoot these things?"

Hardin worked a plug of tobacco, then spat in the cuspidor. It hit with a sharp *ping!*

" 'Spect so."

"Mr. Hardin rode with Jim Lane and Charles Dennison up Missouri ways," Otis said quickly. "Fought Jo Shelby in Bloody Kansas."

Belle tried hard to keep her face composed. Everyone knew Captain Hardin. He'd specialized in interrogating prisoners and had been for a time the most feared man in both Kansas and Missouri.

"Ever go up against them James-Younger boys?" Jess asked pleasantly.

"Scum what rode with Quantrill and Bloody Bill?" Again, Hardin chawed his plug and rang the spittoon. "Yeah, I knew them."

"Didn't like 'em much?" Frank asked.

"Egg-suckin' trash never impressed me none," Hardin said. He turned toward Jess. "Didn't catch your name?"

"Thomas Howard. This is B. F. Winfrey."

"Let's go fire them guns."

They exited the rear door. The shooting range out back wasn't much. A hundred yards away rose a mound of black basalt, maybe sixty feet high. Otis jogged toward it with a gray shingle.

"I never cared much for them Walkers. You got more stopping power with them, but so what? You lookin' to take down a man, the Peacemaker'll punch his ticket."

"Some men take a lot of killin'," Jess said. "Hear Jesse James carries seventeen bullet holes in him. Cole Younger twenty-six."

"And their clocks ain't stopped," Belle said.

"Cross my sights, I'll stop 'em."

"Well," Jess said, pointing at the Walker Colt, "it was good enough for Captain Sam Walker. He give his name to it."

"Which didn't stop him from gettin' kilt."

"I hear them Peacemakers is kind of fragile," Frank James said. "The cylinder stop, the pawl, the mainspring— something's always goin' wrong."

"Don't stop it from doing its job. You can still rotate the cylinder by hand and thumb the rounds home. Hell, you can even pop the caps by hittin' the hammer with a rock."

"Riflin' twists left," Belle said. "That's why I don't use them. Round'll drift two feet over, say, two hundred yards."

"You a good shot at two hundred yards?" Hardin asked. "That shingle's barely a hundred."

Without waiting for a reply, he drew his Peacemaker and faced the shingle. Arm extended, he cocked the .45. The Colt kicked, and the whitish smoke billowed above the gun.

"You missed, sir," Otis called out. "Half a foot to the left."

Hardin took a full minute to fire the next five rounds. He put three of them into the square, stopping each time to wave away the smoke.

"Like I said, it'll get the job done."

"The round still drifts," Belle said.

"You want to do much pistol shootin' over two hundred yards," Hardin said, "get one of them Buntline Specials. It's got a twelve-inch barrel."

"Ain't Buntline the man what writes them Dime Dreadfuls?" Belle asked.

"Yeah," Hardin said, "knew him personally. He had five of them guns custom-made and handed out to that Dodge bunch—Earp, Masterson, Tilghman, and the rest."

Hardin picked up the Spencer. He shoved a seven-round tube into the magazine butt. Pushing the trigger guard forward, he chambered a round, then eared back the hammer.

Two hundred yards away, Otis set another shingle against the other mound of rock.

The Spencer kicked against Hardin's shoulder. The .56-50 round threw off a vast cloud of black-powder smoke.

It took him nearly a minute to put five out of seven into the square.

Jess, standing behind him, silently loaded the Walker Colt.

"If you'd bought a Winchester," Hardin said, staring at the shingle, "I'd still be shootin'."

"Don't think so," Jess said.

Still standing to Hardin's rear, he raised the big Walker and squeezed off five rounds in less than three seconds. The smoke cloud was both blinding and asphyxiating, but Otis screamed out:

"Great shooting, Sheriff. You put all five in dead center."

Jess handed Hardin the empty gun. "Want to test it yourself, Sheriff?"

When Hardin turned to face Jess, the tall, large-framed man stood hip cocked, with his thumbs hooked in his belt, his right hand near the pistol in his belt.

"You done broke the law, boy," he said.

Otis, realizing what had happened, was now running up to them. "You aren't supposed to fire those guns inside the town limits, Mr. Howard. In fact, Deputy Hardin here has to hold on to them till you're ready to leave town."

"Don't think that'll be necessary," Frank James said.

Belle moved off to the side, and Hardin found himself facing the Jameses.

He was ready. He'd killed men in his day. He'd been bayoneted at Shiloh, gut-shot at Missionary Ridge, and eventually sent west to fight Shelby and Quantrill in Bloody Kansas.

Afterward he'd fought Chiricahuas and owlhooters.

He was ready as he'd ever be.

When they pushed their linen dusters open, Colts were stuffed in their pants, butts out.

"What was that you was sayin'," Jess said, "'bout scum what rode with Quantrill and Bloody Bill? Scum like them Jameses?"

It was them. Hardin knew that now.

He said nothing.

"John J., you gonna be a mighty big man 'round these parts," Belle said, grinning, "when you gets yourself killed by Frank and Jesse James."

He didn't see much hope. He did notice that the Jameses' loading gates were open in order to hold their guns inside their pants. They would want to flip them shut before they fired.

That might give him something of an edge. Not much, but something.

He heard an owl hoot, dim and far away, though maybe it was the mourning of a dove.

"They was all trash," Hardin said, "them Youngers included."

He felt good as his gun cleared the holster, leveled, already cocked and—

Out of the corners of his eyes he saw the woman's duster open wide, as though caught by a gust of wind. Then he heard the reports of the Jameses' Colts, silenced by the twin barrels of the cut-down Greener. His eyes flared with blood before he died.

Otis stared at Hardin, his knees trembling, his own face white as death.

"Otis," Frank asked, "it's time to empty out this store. Tell the customers you're closin' up for the day on Hardin's orders."

Otis couldn't take his eyes off Hardin. He was bleeding like a slaughterhouse pig. Still Otis managed to nod.

"You're stickin' with us," Jess said. "Open your mouth, step out of line, you die like a dog."

Keeping his eyes on Hardin, Otis nodded again. He was afraid to speak, even more afraid to look at the three people who had done this thing—who'd shot Hardin to pieces as casually as if he'd been a shingle out there on the basalt.

"Then let's get movin'," Frank James said. "We got a bank withdrawal to make."

19

The rest of the gang was riding up to the bank in groups of two, when to Bob Ford's amazement, he saw the store across from the bank empty out. The store customers mounted their horses, climbed into their wagons, and departed.

Frank and Belle finally left Abernathy's, followed by Jess. He took Otis with him.

Otis's eyes were huge. His clothes and face were smudged by powder smoke.

Jess waved the rest of the gang over to Abernathy's hitch-rack.

"Lawson," Jess said, "you, Belle, and me are going into that bank. Otis here's comin' in with us. He can tell them boys in there we're serious. Frank's doin' sentry duty with the rest of you boys."

"Let's fan out and try not to look too obvious," Frank said.

Jess untied a carpetbag from his pommel. He and Belle started toward the bank. Lawson took up the rear, leading Otis by the arm.

"That was real cute, Jess," Belle said, "leavin' Frank with our mounts. You don't even trust that crowbait you call outlaws to watch the horses."

"I wouldn't trust 'em to pour piss out of a boot with the instructions written on the heel."

"Too bad," Belle said. "It could get rough in the bank."

"Yeah, them bank boys've gone hardcase on us. That Northfield cashier, I could've shot his *cojones* off, and he still wouldn't't've give up the loot."

"You gonna try something different this time?"

"Ain't no cashier standin' up to this baby."

He slapped the carpetbag. It shook with the thrashing buzz of diamondbacks.

They reached the bank. Through the open windows and door, Belle could see the teller counter and desks.

"Banks make me nervous," Belle said.

"It's all that money inside, just waitin' for you, sayin', 'Come on in, girl, help yourself.' "

"Naw, it's them elbow garters the tellers always wear. Look like tourniquets to me."

"That's so the tellers can't shove greenbacks up their sleeves."

"Looks like their arms ought to turn blue."

"They look like faro dealers to me," Lawson said.

"Tell them to deal us in," Jess said.

But as they approached the door, the bank seemed like anything but a friendly card game. A middle-aged hatchet-faced woman in a long black dress was yelling at the employees.

"Who's the widow woman?" Jess asked Otis, pausing in front of the door.

"Agnes Burnside—the bank president's widow. We just buried him this morning."

"You people are useless," she screamed. "You were useless to my husband when he was alive, and you're useless to me now that he's dead."

"She's a little ill-tempered," Otis said.

"Sounds mean enough to kill Jesus," Belle said.

"Useless!" Widow Burnside shrieked.

"She could eat sticks and rocks like a hydrophobic dog," Jess agreed.

"My late husband was la-a-a-a-ax with you men." Agnes Burnside stretched the word out to five syllables. "And we've all suffered from it—from too much la-a-a-x-i-ty."

"What's laxity?" Lawson asked.

"It's what Belle's takin' all that Lydia Pinkham's for," Jess said. "Maybe we should give her a bottle."

"That tincture of opium'll do it," Belle agreed. "Bind her up tighter'n a gnat's asshole."

Turning around inside the bank, the widow woman saw Belle and her friends.

"Look at this," Agnes said. "Four customers and not one of you is moving to help them."

She pushed a teller toward the counter. The rest of them hurried to their desks.

"Can I help you?" the nervous teller asked Jesse.

Jesse pulled a Navy Colt out of his duster and jumped onto the counter. He fired four shots into the ceiling.

"You can help me by openin' that safe and handin' over your money," Jesse James roared.

20

John Slocum opened a bloodshot eye. Kate Elder was shouting at him from the balcony.

"Hurry up, John. Get your ass over here."

He pulled the pillow over his head and went back to sleep.

Kate crossed the room and yanked the pillow away.

"You got some bullion in our bank?"

"So?"

"Well, there's eight hardcases in dusters standing in front of that bank. I do believe they're robbin' it."

That got Slocum up. He slipped into his gray twill pants and pulled his suspenders up over his naked shoulders. He took his Navy Colt from under his pillow and shoved it into his pants.

There was a round maplewood table with matching bentwood chairs on the balcony, and the midday sun was scorching. He decided he'd best take a seat.

"Now what's this stuff about dusters and hardcases and bank robbers and—?"

Then he saw them in front of the bank.

"Darlin', bring me that carryin' case by the wardrobe. A bottle of that there sour mash, while you're at it."

He continued to study the bank robbers. They were nearly

eight hundred yards away, which was a lot of distance, but still he believed he could shorten it.

In fact, he could shorten it a lot.

Truth was, he planned to salt their tails for them.

He turned to Kate. ''Put the travelin' case on the table, sugar. Looks like I got some work to do.''

21

Sheriff J. P. Powers, decked out in a black frock coat and vest, a white linen shirt, and his best working Stetson, bellied up to the bar of the Longbranch. He had big shoulders and robust health for a man of his age, but returning from the funeral had made him feel old.

His two deps were also dressed in their Sunday best— Wilson in his fringed buckskin jacket, Sam Puckett in a dark coat and vest.

They too had just returned from Henry Burnside's burial.

"Agnes led him one hellacious life," Wilson said, lifting a glass.

"But he's free of her now," Powers said.

He and Puckett joined Wilson in his drink.

The fat, bald-headed barkeep—dressed in a white shirt with rolled-up sleeves and a long white apron—joined them.

"She has a hard heart," said the barkeep, refilling their glasses.

"Say it again," Puckett said.

Powers glanced around the saloon. It was a hot sleepy nothing afternoon. He and his deps were the only three up at the bar. A few cowhands sat at the tables, sipping beer, playing listless games of poker and red dog.

It was too hot to do much else. Even the ladies of the evening depicted in the wall paintings looked hot and tired. Powers hooked a heel on the long brass footrail and leaned against the bar.

"Henry," Wilson said, lifting his shot glass toward heaven, "them employees of yours are gonna miss your ass somethin' fierce."

"Agnes'll rawhide 'em seven ways from sundown," Puckett agreed.

"East, west, and crossways," Powers nodded, joining them in another shot.

"J. P.," Wilson said, "you think we can get free of these monkey suits now?"

"Henry's free," Puckett said. "Why not?"

"We've suffered enough," Wilson said.

"I be your witness there," said Puckett.

Then the shots rang out.

From the bank.

Powers was the first out the batwings and into his saddle. Well mounted on a big sorrel gelding and still dressed in his black frock coat, vest, and Stetson, he pounded leather up the street.

His deps booted their mounts into his dust.

Rounding the town square at a dead run, Powers could now see the bank robbers, milling in front of the bank.

It was then one of the robbers—a tall man in a tan plainsman's hat with either a Sharps or a Spencer, Powers couldn't tell at two hundred yards—shot his horse through the right shoulder.

The sorrel went down like he'd hit a brick wall, throwing Powers free, skidding and tumbling across the dusty Tucson street.

His two deps were now taking cover behind a freight wagon, and Powers scrambled for it himself, bullets kicking dust all around him, his nose bloodied, his clothes ripped and covered with dirt.

Bullets were hammering the wagon as if this were Cemetery Ridge.

"Let's turn this damn thing over," Powers yelled.

Cutting the mules free, they put their backs in it.

Just as it flipped over, a .56-caliber round backed by fifty grains of black powder took Wilson off at the right knee.

While Puckett made him a belt tourniquet, Powers attempted to squeeze off two shots.

"Jesus," Puckett screamed at him, "you were a dozen yards short."

"It's these damn carbines," Powers screamed back. "They ain't got the range. We need real rifles."

"They're back in the office, remember? Under lock and key? The town council made us confiscate them."

"They wanted a gun-free town," Powers said.

"It ain't gun-free no more," Puckett shouted. "Them bank robbers got a whole arsenal."

The outlaws' bullets thundered against the wagon like Armageddon.

22

"Drag that damn stagecoach over here," Frank James shouted at his men. "We need some cover."

His duster pockets were filled with a dozen extra tubes, so reloading his weapon was quick and simple. Crouched on one knee, he could lay round after round into the top of the sheriff's turned-over wagon, the big Spencer smoking and kicking against his shoulder.

If Powers wanted to poke his carbine over that wagon bed, it would cost him.

It had already cost his dep a knee.

When the boys returned with the coach, he set Emilio by the end gate and told him to continue the covering fire. He thought he'd give the Spencer a rest.

While his boys peppered the sheriff, Frank paused to study the stage. It was an Abbot & Downing Special, the best coach made. Its woodwork was choice hickory, and it had steel axles and springs as well as brass fittings. Its heavy leather seats could carry fifteen people comfortably.

Hmmmm, he thought. The dray horses look rested. If Jess hurries with that loot, we might just escape in the stage.

It'd be nice to visit Mexico in style.

23

John Slocum opened his long hardwood traveling case on the balcony table. Inside was a disassembled Sharps. Its component parts were kept in custom-fitted slots.

Slocum locked the long, diagonally packed octagonal barrel into the breech. He slid in the trigger housing and breechblock, then screwed in the foregrip, stock, and butt plate.

He mounted a twelve-power sniper scope over the breech.

In the case he kept six cartridges. He lined them up on the table. Six 700-grain slugs backed by 170 grains of black powder. A single round would drop a bull elephant.

It'd make a mess of a man.

He shoved the trigger guard forward, jammed a cartridge into the breech, and swung the lever shut.

Squinting into the scope, he studied his line of fire. His chair was a little high relative to the balcony railing, on which he intended to steady the rifle.

"Honey," Slocum said to Kate, "bring me a couple of them pillows."

He stood up while she placed them on his chair. Turning the chair around, he sat down again. Bracing his arms on the chair's bentwood back, he lay the long octagonal barrel on the black iron balcony.

There. That was just right.

He found his focus on a brightly embroidered black sombrero with a big floppy brim. The man wearing it was turned away from Slocum, shooting at the pinned-down posse further up the street.

Slocum thought it was time to give law and order a hand.

The cross hairs converged on the back of the Mexican's hat.

24

Frank James's eyes stung from the black-powder smoke. Taking off his bandanna, he turned away from Emilio and, staring up the street, started to wipe them.

Approximately 750 yards up Main, Frank caught a glint of light. It was up on the balcony of the Light of Love Parlor House. The glint was suddenly shrouded by a white cirrus cloud of smoke, which burst into flame.

Frank stood stock-still.

There was no point in ducking.

The flight time of the Sharps "Big Fifty" slug, traveling 750 yards, is slightly under two seconds, so Frank had a rough idea what would happen next. When the slug slammed into the back of Emilio's head—seven hundred grains of soft, decelerating lead moving at six hundred feet per second—Frank was stunned but not surprised.

A man's head is a hard, heavy object, and a projectile as soft as a bullet will, at that speed, flatten like a pancake on impact. So the bullet did not enter the back of Emilio's head as a slug but as something saucer shaped.

It ripped off the top of his skullcase, then tore out his forehead and eyes.

Frank's major impression was, however, of Emilio's brains. He saw his brains go—huge coils of snaky gray matter, blood soaked, mixed with fragments of the cranium, spilling across the street.

The sound of the shot traveled slower than the decelerating lead, so the blast did not reach them until three-fourths of a second after the projectile actually hit.

In fact, Emilio's brains were scattered all around them before they actually heard the shot.

Tucson is surrounded on all sides by high peaks, so when the noise reached them, it came as a *BOOM!* that lasted for seconds before it was reverberated into many smaller *boom-boom-boom*s, that echoed like rolling thunder through the mountains, crashed, then cracked repeatedly like packets of firecrackers, rattled softly, faded, and were gone.

Frank went straight to his horse. In his saddlebags were a pair of binoculars. He wanted a look at the man with the Sharps.

He had a feeling they had met before.

25

Jess stood over the cashier, a boot heel on his throat, a Walker Colt in his mouth.

Lawson was pistol-whipping the teller, now spread-eagled over the bank counter.

Both captives' mouths and noses were filled with blood.

"What do you mean," Jess screamed at the cashier, "you don't know the combination?"

Jess opened the loading gate. He ejected the single bullet, reinserted it into the Colt, and spun the cylinder.

"What's the goddamn combination?" Jess roared.

"I don't know," the man said. "Jesus God, I don't know."

Again, he shoved the barrel into the cashier's mouth, eared back the hammer, and pulled the trigger.

When it snapped on an empty cylinder, the man's bladder released.

"What he means," Agnes Burnside shouted, as she walked up to Jess and stuck a finger in his face, "is that Tucson people aren't redneck trash like you Missouri scum. We're made of sterner stuff. You ask me, it's no wonder you lost the war. Your terrorist methods did not work up there, and they will not work here. Torturing defenseless men! Threatening innocent women! What will you do for an encore? Butcher babies?"

"Lady," Belle said, "cut the shit."

"You watch your foul mouth," Agnes raged. "That's another thing Tucson people do not tolerate—profanity. Nor do we tolerate the likes of you—you Strumpet of Sodom, Whore of Gomorrah, Harlot of Babylon, you—"

"Aw, hell," Belle said wearily.

Turning off a pivot, she hit Agnes as hard as she knew how, getting everything she had behind the punch.

Jess shook his head. "Now what'd you have to hit her in the mouth for? Break her jaw she won't be able to spit out the combination."

"I couldn't stand it no more," Belle said.

"I couldn't take it no more neither," said Lawson.

"Well, sit her up and tie her down." They propped her up in an armchair, lashing her wrists to the arms.

When Belle threw a pitcher of water in her face, Agnes came to.

"You foul slut!" Agnes shrieked.

When Belle reared back for a second roundhouse, Jess grabbed her wrist.

"I said don't break her jaw."

"Then *do* something."

He nodded wearily.

It was time for his snake.

To Belle's dismay, she suddenly noticed there was no more gunfire.

Looking out the window, she saw Emilio lying facedown in the street.

Jess had the diamondback out of its case and was fooling with the leather hood on its head. Its tail sounded like a locust horde.

"Jess," Belle said, "hurry up with that rattler."

"Yeah," Lawson said, peeking out the window, "I think we got trouble."

26

Sheriff Powers didn't have the slightest interest in who the sharpshooter was. All he cared about was the express wagon across the town square. If he and Puckett could make it across the square, using those three clumps of cottonwoods for cover, they could flip that wagon over and return the outlaws' fire with their carbines.

"Wilson," Powers said, "you got to hold tight. Me and Pucket are gonna haul ass 'cross that square and pin down them robbers."

He lashed Wilson's belt-and-carbine tourniquet tight against his thigh with a second belt, then propped Wilson up against the wagon bottom.

Wilson's face was white as a winding sheet, but he managed a terse nod.

"You get them sonsofbitches," Wilson said.

"We'll try."

Puckett looked less enthusiastic.

"Puckett," Powers said, "let's do it."

"For thirty dollars a month?"

"Yessir."

The big Sharps spoke again from almost a half mile away, and another outlaw fell.

With Puckett in tow, Powers dogtrotted across the square.

27

Slocum's right thumb slammed the trigger guard forward. Ejecting the spent shell, he shoved a fourth round into the smoking breech.

"Darlin', pour me another shot of that Jackson's Sour Mash."

Kate Elder strolled stark naked out onto the balcony, pouring herself a shot on the way. She placed the bottle on the table near his elbow. She kept the glass.

"Fella shoots men like tin cans don't need no glass."

"Get me another cee-gar while you're at it."

She brought the box. Flicking a phosphorus-tipped lucifer with her thumbnail, she lit the Havana for him. Inhaling deeply, she stepped in front of him and placed the Havana between his teeth.

"Anything else?"

"Yeah, get out the way. You're obstructin' my view."

Slowly, hips swaying, she lowered herself to her knees. She looked up at him with mischievous eyes. Several strands of red hair were stuck against her pouty bee-stung lips. Her fingers toyed with the buttons on his fly.

"This far enough out the way?" she asked.

"Don't make no sudden moves."

He jammed the breechblock shut, chambering a round.

Pressing his cheek against the wood stock, he stared back into the scope.

"Mmmmmm," she said, undoing the last of the buttons. "What do we have here?"

She moved in for a closer inspection.

28

The sniper's fourth round ripped through Dick Bane's right eye, sending his Stetson flying.

Frank glared at his gang, cowering on the ground.

"Get up, goddamn you," Frank shouted. "He'll shoot you on the ground sure as on your feet."

When the gang still groveled, Frank raised his Spencer and levered rounds into the dirt around them, under their arms, and between their legs. He shouted:

"Get up and grab that buckboard over there. It'll give us some cover. Hurry, before he has time to reload."

The remaining outlaws trotted toward the buckboard. The two buggy horses were now kicking and bucking. They had to cut the animals loose in order to move the wagon.

Smoke blossomed over the Light of Love, and Planck went down as if he'd been kicked by a mule.

"Who *are* you?" Frank James said half aloud, putting the binoculars to his eyes.

But he saw nothing.

The man on the balcony was still shrouded in smoke.

29

Lawson tied the wrists and feet of the pistol-whipped cashier to the legs of a heavy oak office chair. Jess approached the bloody man, holding the diamondback's head in one fist, its midsection in the other.

The snake was over eight feet in length and thick as a man's forearm. Its segmented tail thrashed across the floor, and its forked tongue flicked in and out. Its hiss and ratcheting rattle no longer sounded like those of a single snake but reverberated like the buzzing of an entire den.

The snake's blazing eyes with their yellow, vertically distended pupils seemed almost supernaturally evil, and when Jess placed the diamondback alongside the banker's throat—so close the darting tongue flicked his Adam's apple—the man's bladder discharged a second time.

"Give it up, friend," Jess said. "The combination. That old woman ain't worth it."

"Jess," Lawson said. "I don't think he knows it."

"I ain't so sure," Belle said. "Let me try it."

Jess started to hand her the diamondback when the snake exploded and broke free. *Crotalus adamanteus,* the most feared snake in North America, was thrashing across the bank floor.

Jess and Belle leaped up onto the counter, while Lawson bolted out the door.

The diamondback slithered between chairs and spittoons, coat trees and desks, moving with a flowing slippery grace, every inch of its diamond-marked body squirming and writhing. The high-pitched rattles screamed like banshees and the snake's wedge-shaped head levitated above the twisting body, the wild eyes flashing, the four-inch dripping fangs folding and unfolding from the roof of its mouth, the thin tongue darting in and out.

Agnes and Harold—still trussed to their chairs—managed to scoot across the room to the far corner, but the snake followed, coiling in front of them.

It struck Harold in the crotch, so hard that its fangs snagged in his pelvis and pants like fishhooks.

Harold howled like a baying dog, convulsed, and then passed out.

Screams pumped out of Agnes's body over and over and over.

Jess and Belle grabbed the befouled Harold and pitched him, his snake, and the chair through the big front window.

Belle rushed to reopen Jess's carpetbag. She took out a second diamondback, its head and rattles muffled by leather hoods.

"There, there, baby," Belle cooed to the thrashing rattler. "Mama's gonna take good care of her baby. Just relax."

Agnes's eyes flared and went wild. Her body convulsed, racked by more screams.

Belle removed the snake's two hoods and started toward the widow.

"Come on, sugar," Belle purred to the diamondback. "Don't be afraid. Everything's gonna be fine. Guess what we got for dinner."

30

Powers and Puckett had just upended the express wagon when Harold's body went tumbling out the window, the dead diamondback dangling from his crotch.

Powers made up his mind.

"Puckett, help me cut the lead jack out of the traces. I'll also want the next four animals on a jerk line."

Puckett stared at Powers, not moving.

Powers shook him by the arm. Reluctantly, Puckett started cutting out the mules.

"If I can get around them boys and reach the jail," Powers said, "I can badge and arm a dozen men. We can stop them."

"That'll leave me here alone."

"They ain't comin' this way. This square's a dead end."

"But the fella with the Sharps?"

"Something's silenced him. Hell, he's just one man anyhow. He's gonna need help."

Powers swung onto the lead jack, bareback. He booted him toward the outlaws, the other four mules following his dust.

31

Slocum swung the trigger guard forward. He had one round left. He had thought about saving it.

Then he saw the sheriff charge the outlaws on mule-back.

The one on the board sidewalk—who had just run out of the bank—had a clear shot at Powers, and he was going to take it. Slocum couldn't let that happen. He shoved his last cartridge into the smoking breech and slammed the lever home.

He shot the outlaw between the shoulder blades.

Through his whitish gunsmoke, he saw Powers tear past the turned-over stage. The old man roweled his mule till blood flowed, and, at last, all five mules were galloping past the bandits.

Frank James, however, shoved another tube into his Spencer and climbing up on the stage, raised his rifle.

The first of Powers's mules he shot through the back of the neck.

The second through the head.

The third shot he rushed but he still hit the jenny's rear hock, upending her ass-over-teakettle.

Powers was pressed flat against the jack's neck, but even so, the fourth round had enough steam to graze the back of his head, then kill his mount through the neck.

Powers and the mule went down in an explosion of dust. The second jenny to the rear thundered into them, breaking both forelegs.

The fallen mules formed a crude wedge, aimed toward the bank robbers. When the dust cleared, Slocum saw Powers, who'd been thrown clear, crawling into the lee of the braying animals, dragging his carbine behind him.

He appeared to have fractured a hip.

32

Frank now had three men left with him, and they were hysterical.

"I ain't hangin' 'round here to get shot to hell!" One-Eye shouted. "That dude with the Sharps is blowin' us to pieces."

"Ain't you forgettin' the money?" Frank asked.

The three men swung onto their mounts. Noches pointed at the five corpses spread-eagled in the dirt.

"Tell them about the *dinero*."

"You're leavin' your friends in that bank," Frank said.

"They ain't no kin to me," One-Eye said. He hocked and spat at Frank's feet.

Frank looked at Zapata. "He can shoot you off that bay easy as on the street," Frank said.

"Then I shall die on my horse" Zapata said, "not in the dirt like *una perro*."

Wheeling their mounts around, they charged up the street.

33

The head of the jenny and the jack's rump formed a crude
V. Powers waited inside of it. He steadied his carbine on
the jack's rump and watched the three horsemen over his
sights.

He did not know how much time he had. He'd broken
his hip when the jack went down, and his head felt like
someone had taken an ore hammer to it. He was in shock,
and any time now he could pass out.

He figured he could get off three shots.

The sights on his Winchester were set for two hundred
yards, but his vision was blurred and he would have to let
them get closer. Also, there was a sharp breeze from the
east, and he would have to allow for windage.

Worst of all, the men were slung low in their saddles,
their chests obscured by their horses' necks.

Powers would have to go for head shots.

He went for the middle outlaw first. At one hundred yards
the carbine would pull high, so Powers—ignoring the man's
gunfire—aimed just to the right of the man's chin. He held
his breath and squeezed. The man's forehead exploded in
a bright burst of blood.

The force of the wind had streaked the next outlaw's face

with red dust. His filthy sweat-stained Stetson had blown down the back of his neck, the hat's cord tearing at his throat. Powers fixed his sights to the right of the tight cord.

At seventy-five yards the carbine would shoot high.

The carbine kicked, and Powers blew away the top of the man's head, his Stetson going with it.

He levered another round. He was nauseous with pain, and time was running out.

The rider was less than fifteen yards away, pistol drawn, and bullets were flying all around Powers.

Suddenly, the man's gun jammed. He sat straight up and reached for a second horse pistol.

Powers put the sights squarely on his chest, but then rushed the shot. He hit the horse instead—between the eyes, dropping him dead in his tracks.

The man went flying over the head of his falling mount, crashing into Powers like an express train, knocking him out cold.

Powers came to—to find One-Eye was standing over him, covered with blood and dust. The outlaw's left arm was fractured and hanging useless, but in his right fist was a cocked Colt.

"You got some hard bark on you, old man. That dep of yours wouldn't lift his head long enough to fire a round, but you kept throwin' lead."

Powers hocked and spat at the man's feet. His sputum was tinged with blood. He was so whipped down he couldn't see the man's face.

Still he got it out.

"Kiss my ass, you scum-suckin' sonofabitch."

"Old man, it's gonna be one hellacious pleasure puttin' you down."

The man bent over him, yanked the Winchester out of his powerless hands, and flung it up the street. He placed the cocked Colt between Powers's eyes.

"Remember me when the lights go out."

34

Slocum studied One-Eye over the sights of his slip-hammered Navy Colt. At 150 yards a round would drop a good six feet. He was operating at twice his gun's effective range.

But when the man put the pistol to Powers's head, Slocum had no choice.

He let the hammer down.

And shot out the bandit's last good eye.

35

The bank door was flung open. Through the entranceway, Frank could see Agnes, still decked out in her widow's weeds, tied to a chair. At her feet was coiled a spitting, buzzing diamondback.

Her two surviving employees stood on the counter and screamed.

Jess and Belle bounded out the door. Jess was waving two large grain sacks stuffed with loot. While he tied the bags to the pack mule Belle pointed at all the dead bodies.

"What was this? Little Roundtop?"

"Some fancy man up in that whorehouse got himself a Big Fifty," Frank said. "Cut us to pieces."

"Only one man I knew could shoot like that," Jess said.

"John C. Slocum," Frank said.

"You mean the one what rode with Quantrill and Bill Anderson, when we—," Belle started to say.

"The same," Frank said.

"Anyone else with him?" Belle asked.

Frank raised the binoculars. He stared at the back of the hooker's bobbing head.

"You wouldn't believe me if I told you," Frank said.

"Let's vamoose," said Jess.

"This town ain't healthy," Belle said, still eyeing the corpses.

"Take your time," said Frank, looking through the binoculars. "The sheriff's lost his carbine, and all Slocum's got left is a Colt. The town's weaponless."

"Slocum's the best man with a belt gun I ever seen," Jess said. "Either hand."

"No problem," Frank said. "I got a Spencer now. You two go first, and I'll pin him down. When you get past him, hold him for me with your Winchester."

"That's what I call strategical thinking," Jess said.

"Too bad them good ole boys in the street didn't think of it," Belle said.

"They was in too big a hurry," said Frank.

36

Over his shoulder Powers could hear the man in the balcony shout to him:

"Run for it! You're out of guns."

Powers fished a .41-caliber Remington derringer out of his coat pocket. It was an over-and-under double-barrel with a stud trigger and a hook handle.

"Crawl if you have to," Slocum shouted. "I'll cover you."

Powers turned his head and flashed the stranger a tight smile. He waved the palmed derringer at him, just to let him know he wasn't defenseless.

Slocum grinned back, and suddenly Powers remembered him. Damn it, why hadn't he recognized him up in the room? Probably too busy starin' at that bare-naked female. Why, Slocum had been one of Quantrill's boys.

Yes, Powers remembered him now. Slocum had been one of the good ones—maybe the only good one considerin' the way the others turned out. He was the one what tried to warn Lawrence Town of the massacre, but who got shot in the back by his own friends 'fore he could get there, shot down like a dog.

That man up there wasn't no Quantrill trash. He was all right. Just look at the way he done them what backshot him just now. Salted their tails proper. Powers grinned through split lips. Who said there weren't no justice?

Powers started to laugh but choked and then spat bloody sputum.

Still he managed to wave at Slocum a second time.

"I knew you was with Quantrill," Powers rasped, "but you was okay."

"I remember you too, old man. You was hell on wheels even then."

Slocum lifted his bottle of Jackson's Sour Mash and offered a toast.

"Wish I could give you some of this," Slocum said.

"We'll split a barrel later."

"Just watch your line of fire. Here they come—bigger'n Beelzebub, howlin' for your hide."

The old man kissed his derringer for luck and crouched low behind the jack.

37

"Get back," Slocum yelled to Kate, who was hunkering down beside him.

He studied the approaching riders through his detached sniper's scope. Jess, Frank James and Belle Starr were roaring down on him like hell's fury, and he wasn't sure which one was the worst.

In a close-up fight he figured Jess.

If it took some thinking, Frank.

For pure meanness, Belle.

Frank came to a halt two hundred yards up the street. He swung down off his gray, lifted the far, rear hock, and put a shoulder into the animal's hindquarters. With a bone-jarring *thud!* one thousand pounds of horse crashed onto the dusty street. Whipping his Spencer out of his saddle sheath, he lay behind his fallen mount.

And started levering rounds at Slocum.

Rounds were banging and screaming off the black iron balcony, spraying sparks, and ricocheting through the windows. Inside, they shattered the triptych mirror of the Louis Quinze cherrywood vanity, knocked Turner's *Slave Ship* off the wall, and rang the bed's brass struts like chimes.

Slocum had never had the priviledge of facing twenty thousand charging Yankees on Missionary Ridge, but he had been trampled at Shiloh and had been one of the last half-dozen rebs stampeded out of Vicksburg.

This wasn't exactly the same.

Still, it had its moments.

The worst part was that he couldn't touch the enemy.

Belle and Jess rode past unchallenged while Slocum dived behind the bed with Kate.

38

Jess and Belle kept Slocum's balcony covered with rifle fire while Frank swung onto the gray. He trotted up to the old man, keeping his Spencer on him the whole time.

"Well, Major Red Leg, you ain't so high and mighty now, are you?"

"Goddamn you to hell."

"That He will, lawman. He definitely will. But you'll get there first."

The heavy Spencer kicked. A .56-50 round shattered Powers's left shoulder.

Powers flopped on his right side with a sobbing gasp.

"Left you kind of lopsided, didn't I?" Frank said. "Maybe we can balance it a little."

Frank levered the trigger guard and broke Powers's right shoulder.

Powers screamed and convulsed.

The gray stopped directly over Powers. Frank's Spencer was pointed at Powers's gut.

"Keep hell hot for me," Frank James said, "you jayhawkin' sonofabitch."

Building the Pyramids might have been hard, laying the first transcontinental railroad might have been harder still, but for Powers, lifting the .41-caliber derringer was the hardest thing he'd ever done.

Pulling the stud trigger was the easy part.

Frank's upper chest bloomed with blood, and his face was filled with shocked surprise.

Powers managed a tight smile.

Before Frank could return fire, Slocum crawled out onto the balcony and shot the hat off the outlaw's head.

The gray, starting at the smell of Frank's blood, vaulted Powers and took off.

Slocum scrambled back to the bedroom under a withering storm of fire.

39

By the time Slocum reached the street, people were peeking out of windows and doors, and the gang was gone.

Kneeling beside Powers, Slocum held his head. Holding the whiskey bottle to his mouth, he dribbled some on his lips. Powers opened his eyes.

"Told you we'd have a drink," Slocum said.

The old man licked his lips. "Ought to throw you in jail. You hid two guns from me."

"But I brought you this bottle."

"That's a fact. Got any more?"

Slocum dribbled some on his mouth.

"Cuts the dust," Powers said.

The old man stared at him. The stare held Slocum hard and did not let him go.

"You'll do," the old man said.

No one had said that to Slocum, not in a long time.

"Take it easy," Slocum said.

"You ain't got time to take it easy. Them boys what took your gold, they're gettin' away."

"The gold don't mean nothing."

"Them friends of yours what died for it. They meant something."

110

''Sure, but them Jameses play for keeps. There'll be more of them with their remuda.''

''They were your friends, you said, the ones in the mine, the ones what died.''

''But—''

''Some things you don't leave undone.''

The old man convulsed. Blood filled his mouth and nose. He died.

Slocum pulled himself to his feet.

Some things you don't leave undone.

Slocum got up and headed for the jail.

It was time to pick up the rest of his guns.

Part 5

There's no Sunday in Sonora,
no law in Chihuahua,
and no God at all in Mala Cruz.

—John Henry "Doc" Holliday

40

At last, the coughing subsided. John Henry "Doc" Holliday returned the bloodstained handkerchief to his back pocket. His face was white as death.

He took off his wrinkled black serge coat and hung it on a wall peg. He'd obviously lost a lot of weight, and the coat fit his frame like a sack. He removed a gold-plated Hunter from his vest pocket, its key dangling from the gold chain. He clicked it open.

"It's eight thirty-five P.M., Wednesday. How long that bullet been in there?"

"Over five days," Frank James said.

Frank was naked from the waist up and lay spread out on a wooden table. His chest wound made sucking noises.

"Took us a while to lose that posse," Belle Starr explained.

Doc Holliday sighed. He clicked the lid shut, then put the watch and chain in his vest pocket. He rolled up the sleeves of his white linen shirt, walked over to a pitcher and bowl, and washed his hands with yellow soap.

He went back to the wooden table and helped himself to a shot from Frank's bottle. He tossed it back, then helped himself to another.

Frank James studied the doctor with misgivings. Holliday

was a lunger with a drinking problem, and the old mining shack was hardly an antiseptic hospital. Nothing about his present situation looked good.

"Whiskey won't make that consumption feel better," Frank said.

"It'll make *me* feel better," Holliday said.

"Talk like that," Frank said, "makes me wonder what kind of doctor you are."

"He's the best you're gonna get 'round here," Bob Ford said. "The territory ain't noted for medical science."

Belle relieved Holliday of his bottle and helped herself to a drink.

Holliday gave Ford a slow stare. The ginger-haired man was barely twenty, of medium height, and had acne scars. He wore the same dusty trail garb as Frank and Belle and had hard eyes.

Holliday didn't like him.

"Ain't much of a hole," Frank James said, pointing to his chest wound. "A stingy gun was all. I been shot by worse. In Northfield took a rifle ball in the foot."

"That's a forty-one-caliber slug in your lung," Holliday said. "I'm gonna have to dig it out and stick hot metal to the hole. If you make it, you can figure a month in this shack 'fore you're fit to ride."

"We got some hard travelin', Doc," Frank said. "Mejico's callin'."

"What's the hurry?" Holliday asked, sterilizing his forceps with trade liquor.

"Ninety-proof whiskey, two-hundred-proof women, and twenty-four-carat gold," Frank said.

"Travel with that shot-up lung," said Holliday, "all you'll get is a hundred proof dead."

"I got to chance it, Doc," Frank said.

"Hemorrhagin' to death ain't much of a chance," said Holliday. "Lobar pneumonia ain't no hand to draw to neither."

"We're talkin' *muchos pesos,* Doc," Belle said.

"You're talkin' Mala Cruz? The Evil Cross?" Holliday asked.

"How'd you know?" Frank asked.

They were all shocked that he'd guessed their rendezvous.

"Where else would you be safe from both the U.S. marshals and the *federales?"* Holliday said. "It's where all the owlhooters been hidin' out. Just got back from there myself last night. Had to cool off a spell after that Clanton fracas."

"Is it like they say?" Bob Ford asked.

"There's no Sunday in Sonora, no law in Chihuahua, and no God at all in Mala Cruz."

"Heard like Mala Cruz was a good place to raise kids," Belle sneered.

"If your kids are Bill Hickok and Coleman Younger," Holliday said.

"Or Jesse James," Bob Ford smiled.

"Jess never made it," Doc said.

The three of them froze.

"He got cornered outside of Santa Madre by *federales."*

"Where is he now?" Frank asked.

"He went to where they hand out the free room and board. Hard time in a stone hotel. A man named Thomas Howard's doin' five years straight up in a hell hole called La Fortaleza. The Fortress. A slave-labor gold mine owned by Díaz himself."

"I got to get to him," Frank said.

"There ain't no hurry," Holliday said. "You'll know just where to find him." Holliday turned to Frank with the scalpel and forceps in one hand, a bottle of whiskey in the other. "Drink as much of this as you can stand now."

"I said I got to get to him," Frank said.

"He's got our gold," said Belle.

"And I said take your time. Jess ain't goin' no place. But you might be. You'll be goin' straight to hell if we don't get that slug out."

"You're already white as a windin' sheet," Belle said.

"But—" Frank started to object.

"You're no help to Jess dead," Bob Ford said.

"Anyway," Holliday said, "don't be so down at the mouth. We get this bullet out, maybe I'll be takin' you down to Mala Cruz myself."

"You got an idea for gettin' Jess out of that prison?" Frank asked.

"More'n an idea," Holliday said.

"You got some kind of plan," Belle said.

"Do I have a plan for you," Holliday said.

Frank shook his head, but then lifted the bottle.

He didn't have much choice.

41

The day following surgery, Holliday left his recovering patient for a quick visit to Tombstone. He stopped by the Western Union telegraph office. Before entering, he paused to reread a note Kate Elder had sent him.

Know a man what wants to meet the James Gang.
Frank needs a doc, and
They might be come to you. This man can help them
get Jess out of La Fortaleza. And help us both
get rich. Tell me where we should meet.

Holliday reconsidered the offer, then composed a short wire addressed to Kate Elder.

Two words, that was all. Two words.

MALA CRUZ.

42

John Slocum got up from his all-night poker game and stretched. He'd been bucking the tiger for nine straight hours and needed a break.

"Deal around me, boys," Slocum said, heading toward the cantina bar.

Hooking a boot heel on the long brass rail, he ordered a shot of mescal. He didn't feel too bad. He'd hit Mala Cruz with two hundred dollars in his oiled-silk money belt and with Kate Elder at his side. In ten days he'd parlayed that stake into two thousand and Kate had made almost a grand working the upstairs cribs.

The cards were not only running his way, the cantina suited him. He'd certainly seen worse. The Culebra de Cascabel (the Rattlesnake Den), if nothing else, had a real bar of darkly stained oak, not pinon planks nailed to whiskey kegs. The liquor was actually drinkable, not Injun whiskey concocted from alcohol, tobacco juice, black powder, cayenne, and diamondback venom. The piano was not painfully out of tune.

Yes, if Slocum had to hang around Mejico, waiting for the Jameses, the Rattlesnake was as good a hellhole as any. This was no pole-and-'dobe lean-to. The Rattlesnake had high ceilings with a score of gambling tables lining the walls. The room reverberated with the rattle of the dice and the slap of the pasteboards. The air was thick with the smells of beer, whiskey, cigars, and women.

Mostly Slocum like the smells of the perfumed ladies. In fact, the middle of the second floor had been knocked out, creating a four-sided interior balcony with a huge rectangular hole in the center. Along the overhead railings stood the Rattlesnake's dozen-odd hookers displaying their wares. The doxies were decked out in skimpy corsets, garish garters, and net stockings. They liked to keep a leg cocked on the lower rail, while their unrestrained bosoms dangled provocatively over the top rail. If you made eye contact, you were greeted by whistles and catcalls inviting you to come up and try them out.

The rickety staircase did a land-office business.

Slocum studied the whores. He'd heard a new *gringa puta* had joining their ranks. So far he had not seen her.

"Gimme the bottle," Slocum said, turning around to face the bar.

The barkeep was a big Texan named Rio, wearing a white apron over a gingham shirt, a bowler hat on his head.

"Pour one for yourself," Slocum said.

"*Salud y pesetas.*" Health and wealth, Rio said.

"*Y cojones.*" And balls, Slocum answered.

They each threw back their shots.

"How's the new girl?" Slocum asked him, pouring himself another.

"Meaner'n a chain-gang dog."

"I meant in bed."

"I meant in bed."

Slocum turned around to face the cantina. A *mejicana* whore with waist-length hair black as polished ebony, wearing a red corset and garters, pounded out "La Paloma" on the piano, banging the loud pedal on the refrain. Slocum sipped his mescal, watched the hookers work the crowd, and listened to the lilting *mejicano* ballad. He said to the bartender over his shoulder:

"How's the piano player?"

"A little slow. She was born with shiny black hair instead of brains."

"Most of the whores 'round here are hotter'n a hickory fire."

"Yeah, starvation's a great aphrodisiac."

"Sounds like I should take a pass on the new girl?" Slocum asked.

"If pussy had teeth, she could eat rocks."

"She ought to be in that card game over there," Slocum said.

They both watched the card players. Rio worked his plug of tobacco, then spat in a cuspidor.

"Think a couple of them's flashin' signals," Slocum said. "Sharin' information, then splittin' the take later."

"You cut their sign," the barkeep said, "you'll read *their* hands. Bust them out big time."

"That's what I'm hopin'," Slocum said. "Bust them down to suckin' eggs."

"Bust them down to nothing."

Slocum picked up his bottle and turned toward a table.

"Best get something to eat," he said to Rio over his shoulder. "Got to keep up my strength."

"Why? Gonna try out that new girl? I 'spect she's your type."

"What *is* my type?" Slocum asked.

"Eight to eighty. Blind, crippled, or crazy."

"Sounds like hard trade, you ask me," Slocum said, shaking his head.

"Just the way you like them."

"Yeah, just what I need. A hard whore."

"That's right, *amigo*. *Una puta dura*. Mean enough to kill a rock."

43

Slocum sat down at a corner table and had one of the whores hustle him up two antelope steaks, pinto beans, and a half-dozen tortillas. He considered coffee, but he had tried that once.

After his hunger was satisfied, he thought about taking the piano *puta* up to one of the cribs. However, Kate had been giving him a hard eye half the night.

It'd been a week since he had taken her to bed.

Slocum rolled a quirly, twisted the ends, then popped a lucifer with his thumbnail.

Traveling with Kate, it seemed to Slocum, was an awful lot like marriage.

He glanced overhead, looking for her.

And secretly looking for the new *puta*. He didn't believe half what that bardog said.

Figured he'd have to check it out himself.

There had to be some compensations for hanging around this godforsaken hellhole.

Finally he spotted Kate. Black stockings, black garters, a green corset, and long flame red hair.

She was, once again, staring at him.

He nodded toward his room, and she left the rail.

44

Kate sat, naked, in front of the dressing table mirror when he entered his room. She was brushing out her long red hair.

"Damn thing's a rat's nest," she grumbled.

"A snarl of snakes, you ask me."

"Nobody's askin' you."

Slocum casually checked the loads in his Colt. "Heard anything from Doc?"

"Only what I told you before. He ain't lettin' Frank move till he's fit."

"He did get shot. Saw it myself."

"Yes, there it is," Kate said.

"Then there it is."

She stopped brushing her hair and turned around.

"What can I do you for tonight?" Kate asked.

"How 'bout a little romance?"

"You know how?"

"Do you?"

"Don't shuck an old friend. You're a gambler, and I'm a whore."

Slocum lay back on his bed. "Then I'll let you fly the eagle."

Kate gave him a hard stare. "I can give you a rate on a straight lay."

"I'm keepin' an eye on that door."

"Trustin' soul, ain't you?"

"Something's cockeyed tonight."

"This ain't no convent," she admitted.

"And you ain't no cloistered nun."

"I be your witness there."

"You want a drink first?"

She nodded. He took a mescal bottle and two shot glasses from the bedside table. He poured them each a slug.

"Confusion to our enemies," she said, and tossed it back.

"Thought you'd be grateful I asked you up here," Slocum said.

"Surprised is all—seein' as how there's a new girl around."

"Hear she's mean enough to kill Jesus."

Kate took the bottle from him and knocked back another shot. "Make a glass eye weep and turn out a nun."

She put down her shot glass and climbed into bed. She did kiss John first, something she did with no other customer, a long slow tongue-probing kiss, as soft and loving as she knew how.

Then she unbuckled his belt.

Slocum kept his shoulder holster on, and braced his Winchester "One in One Thousand" on the edge of the bed. He slid his slip-hammered blue-steel Navy Colt out from under the pillow. He rested the ivory-handled butt on his thigh.

In the dresser mirror he watched both the rickety door and Kate's long red tresses as they spread across his lap.

As an afterthought, he levered the Winchester. In his line of work, there was no such thing as being too careful.

He came so hard he almost took his eyes off the bedroom door.

Kate looked up at him, face in hands, her elbows straddling his thighs. Her eyes were no longer sneering but soulful.

"John, you and me could try an honest life."

"You'd square up for *me?*"

"I'd try."

"You didn't do it for Holliday."

"He weren't you, John."

"Don't think I could handle it."

"Ever try?" Kate asked.

"Too expensive," Slocum said, staring pointedly at her crotch. "Payin' for all that pussy'd have me broke in a week."

"Wouldn't charge you if we was hitched."

"Straight tongue?"

"Gospel."

"Didn't think you could pleasure a man less'n there was whip-out."

"You lookin' for one on the house?"

"Just wonder what it would be like bein' married. And gettin' it free."

"Want to find out?"

"Ain't it against your religious beliefs?"

She grinned. "Not if it don't fly or have webbed feet."

"You sure you're better than that new girl?"

"Just watch."

"Heard she's hotter'n a two-dollar pistol."

"I said, watch."

He did.

Guns in his fists, he watched her in his dresser mirror. Her body sprawled across his, her flaming tresses strewn across her back, while she practiced her whore's craft.

He watched it all, everything she did, right up to the moment that he came.

After that, all he watched in the warped dresser mirror were his guns, his eyes, and the rickety bedroom door.

Part 6

You may not believe this, but my personal nature is a violent one.

—R. Covington Watley

45

Picture an arrogant English lord, sitting at a baize-covered card table. His sneer is insolent, his attire expensive. He wears a white planter's hat with a two-foot brim and a black leather hatband, heavily inlaid with silver and turquoise. His white coat and pants are of the finest shantung silk as is his matching ruffled shirt. He wears black Wellington boots.

The man smokes imported tailor-made cigarettes in a sterling silver holder encrusted with rubies. His mouth is twisted in a perpetual sneer, as if he found the world and everyone in it beneath his contempt.

Picture his woman. He refers to her as "Her Ladyship Vanessa J. Hastings, of the Eton Hastings." Somehow it doesn't fit. What kind of "lady" wears tantalizing trousers of blackest buckskin, stretched tightly against her long legs and protuberant derriere? Or scarlet blouses of sheer pongee silk, open to the navel? Does true royalty wear its raven tresses butt length? What of the black scoop-brimmed Stetson pulled down low over her eyes. Does a true lady-of-the-realm swagger around the cantina throwing back shots of tequila, laughing raucously, chain-smoking cigarillos, her wrist quirt of polished ebony leather, with its leaded stock and double-plaited lashes of heavy rawhide and triple poppers on the ends, cracking the tops of her black thigh-high riding boots?

What kind of lady indeed?

Picture the other card players. Take William Bassett and James Pardee, for instance. Neither of these men lays claim to royalty. Bassett is a grizzled trailhand with the weathered tan of a man who has spent too many years squinting into cutting wind and scorching desert sun. He wears a gray collarless shirt with two .45s in the waistband, and a cut-down Navy Colt in a half-breed shoulder rig. His right hand is near the shoulder gun. It is always near the shoulder gun.

James Pardee wears a brown frock coat, a white linen shirt, and a brown Stetson. He is younger than Bassett and clean-shaven. He favors a sandy mustache and matching shoulder-length hair. The outturned butts of his two nickle-plated Remingtons protrude under his open coat. His gray gunfighter's eyes stare through everything and everyone.

One suspects his frock coat conceals enough guns to outfit Crook's Geronimo campaign.

What of Captain Cornelius P. Callahan, the U.S. Cavalry officer? He has clear eyes, light blond hair with an aquiline nose. He wears padded epaulets and an officer's saber. The brim of his black wool campaign hat is pinned up on the side with a small U.S. coat of arms. On the opposite side is an eighteen-inch ostrich plume, and under the crown his yellow-gold chin strap, festooned at the ends with two-inch tassels.

What of Ortega de Vásquez de Gama? This distinguished long-haired gentleman in the white suit and matching sombrero. He has fine features, fine eyes, and is the former owner of some of Mejico's richest silver mines. Unfortunately, he is on the run from Díaz's *federales*. He has had the bad judgment to refuse Díaz his exorbitant *mordida*. He felt 50 per cent of his fortune an extortionate amount.

Now he gambles his last poke of silver in a cantina-whorehouse, while Díaz owns his mines.

What of Pedro Valadarez, Ortega's friend and neighbor, who paid Díaz his *mordida*, only to have his hacienda over-run and his four-hundred-year-old claim to his land expropriated. In his black steeple-crowned sombrero and matching jacket and pants, he is the picture of the perfect *charro* gentleman, one of the *buena gente*, a *gachupin*, a true wearer of the spurs.

And what of the dealer? He wears a suit black as any undertaker's, with a matching Stetson. Speaking of undertakers, he is known to have arranged a few cheap funerals in his day. He wears a black string tie with silver tips clasped by a black obsidian arrowhead. His Navy Colts are ivory handled, the butts sticking out. His ebony gunbelt bristles with shiny brass cartridges.

He is sitting now at the table, lighting up a good Havana. He pours a shot of mescal and tosses it back. He apparently likes it because he pours himself another.

"Well, gents," he says, noisily shuffling the cards, "ready for another game?"

What kind of dealer is this?

What kind of man?

What kind of game?

46

Slocum looked around the table. Lord Watley smirked at him. Watley was seated directly across from Slocum and had spent the night haranguing him about "the rudeness of the ruddy Yanks and their bloody joke of a country."

Having already spent four years fighting that country, Slocum had seen no reason to take exception to his statements. Instead he had taken Watley's money. He estimated he now had fifty-five hundred dollars of it.

Watley gestured toward Slocum with his cigarette holder, and his smirk became a sneer.

"Mr. Slocum, while you were gone, Lady Hastings raised a rather indelicate question about these so-called 'soiled doves.'" Watley nodded toward the upstairs whores. "She seems to value your opinion on the matter."

Bassett chawed his plug of tobacco and hit a nearby spittoon.

"Yeah, Slocum's sampled lots of them there soiled doves," he said.

"And left them a hell of a lot more soiled'n when he found them," Pardee said.

Slocum shrugged and shuffled the deck. He offered the cut to de Gama, who declined.

"Five-card stud," Slocum said. "Ante's five bucks."

He began his patter, quiet commentary, nothing dramatic or deceptive.

"Cards," Slocum said. "Eight to a straight, all clubs, Big Lady, no good." On and on his words flowed, falling with the cards, announcing hands and bets.

Slocum filled a straight and raked in the pot.

"Your luck still holds," Watley observed.

"The tiger's ride," Slocum said.

Slocum filled his shot glass to the rim, shuffled the cards, and offered Captain Callahan the cut. He took it. Slocum dealt himself two aces. Lord Watley and the captain stayed on with ace-king and hearts, raising and cross-raising each other. Slocum tried not to scare them out.

"Mr. Slocum," Lady Hastings said, pausing behind Lord Watley, cracking a boot with her quirt, "what I fail to understand is how these wretched women can *sell* themselves to men, such as *yourself.*"

"Try asking one."

"I would," Lady Hastings said, "but they are so disgustingly *low.*"

"We can't all be to the manor born," Captain Callahan pointed out.

"Thank God!" Watley roared.

Slocum had a third ace in the hole and took the pot.

"Some say whores make the best wives," Pardee said, while Watley glared at Slocum.

"They sure know how to pleasure a man," said Bassett.

"I find them base and vulgar," Lady Hastings said.

"Never know till you try it yourself," said Pardee.

"Might be fun," Bassett said, "gittin' taken off your pedestal, made to feel all them base and vulgar things, and nothin' you can do about it."

"A woman of true quality would never submit to such indignities," Lady Hastings said.

"Maybe that depends on the man," Slocum offered, shuffling the cards.

"The man hasn't been born who could bring me to my knees," Her Ladyship said.

She gave Slocum a hard stare.

"Maybe you ain't met him yet."

Slocum started to deal again, when a long-haired Mexican whore with black stockings and a matching chemise sat on his lap. She put her tongue in his ear and started kissing his mouth.

"Ey, chico," she cooed, "you never take me up to thee cribs no more. What's the matter, *guapo?* You no find me pretty? I love you s-o-o-o much, *amigo,* no shit."

She openly groped his crotch.

"Is it true love," Pardee said to no one in particular, "or the pesos in his pocket?"

Slocum pushed her off his lap. She crashed onto the floor.

"Please, *amigo,*" she whimpered, *"por favor."*

"Go on, git," Slocum said.

She limped away.

"Real ladies can't be bought," Lady Hastings sniffed.

"I know some can be rented for the weekend," said Pardee.

"Only real ladies I ever knew charged two fifty for a straight lay, seven and a half for a half and half," Barrett said.

"Game, anyone?" Slocum asked.

The players nodded.

The next hand Slocum's three kings beat Watley's jacks.

During the next he filled a flush to take Pardee's queen-high straight.

"Ante's five bucks, stud's the game," Slocum said idly. "Everyone in?"

They were.

"Cards," Slocum said. "Pair of deuces. Diamonds. Ten-jack."

The rest folded.

"Knew a man named Slocum once did a stretch in Yuma," Pardee said. "Known to rob a bank or two in his time."

"It's a common name," Slocum said.

"I think our dealer's on the owlhoot," Pardee said. "That right, Mr. Slocum?"

"Not lately," Slocum said.

"Perhaps you're in Mala Cruz for the scenic beauty?" Watley asked.

"Anyone who'd go to Mala Cruz for the scenic beauty," Slocum said, "would go to hell for the nightlife."

Slocum dealt. He picked up his third deuce and had the fourth in the hole.

He beat Watley's straight.

"Man can't win for losin' 'round here," Callahan said.

"Maybe it's time for a change of pace," Slocum said. "Try one of them Daughters of Joy upstairs. Could give you a whole new outlook."

"Could be you're right," Callahan said. "Cash me out, boys."

"I believe you are right," de Gama said. "*Vaya con Dios, Señor Slocum.*" Go with God.

Valadarez left with him.

There were just four players then—Pardee, Bassett, Watley, and himself—and he knew now they were cheating. During the last hand he thought he'd cut their sign. If a man touched his nose, he had a nine. Tapped his teeth, a ten. If he scratched his ass, an ace.

Slocum filled his shot glass and lit a Havana. He leaned back in his chair. He had nearly nine grand in his oiled-silk money belt and another three on the baize.

Two more hands, Slocum would read their signals as easily as he read his own cards.

Yes, John Slocum was going to make out like a bandit. It was going to be a *very* lucrative night.

Then to Slocum's amazement, Lady Hastings sneaked upstairs behind Watley's back toward what looked to be Callahan's room.

47

Captain Callahan lay spread-eagled across the upstairs bed.
His wrists and ankles were lashed to the corner posts. He
was buck naked except for a blue checked bandanna tied
around his neck. Lady Hastings, who remained fully clothed
in her black buckskin trousers and matching silk blouse,
paced the side of the bed studying him. Her Stetson was
pulled down over her eyes, and she casually cracked her
boot tops with her quirt.

"I say, ducks," Her Ladyship said pleasantly, "it's aw-
fully sporting of you to join me in my little game."

"Awful sportin' of you to lay all them greenbacks on
me. I ain't never been paid for it before."

"Still and all, I don't see how I can take off my clothes
and climb into that bed with you gaping at me unmention-
ables. I mean, that just wouldn't do. Would it?"

"I could promise not to look."

"I have a better idea."

Her Ladyship solemnly untied the blue checked bandanna
from around the captain's neck and fastened it around his
eyes.

Almost as an afterthought, she plucked one of his wool
socks off the floor and, grabbing him by the nose, wadded
it into his mouth.

48

Watley was furious. Despite his best efforts to cheat the man, Slocum was beating the pants off him. He was beating him with high cards, low cards, and everything in between.

And those few times when Watley—or his cohorts—had the cards, Slocum folded, yielding nothing more than his ante.

He was beating them with humiliating regularity.

Something Watley could not tolerate.

"Tell me, Bassett," Watley asked, "what would you guess to be Mr. Slocum's driving passion? What touches his heart and snares his soul?"

"'Sides pussy, tequila, and the Confederate flag?"

"You left out money," Slocum said.

"My sentiments exactly," Watley said.

"You like that long green?" Slocum asked.

"I thrill to the till's chiming ring."

Slocum shuffled and offered Pardee the cut. He dealt.

"Cards," Slocum said. "Two aces, three-four, a deuce, and a five. Oh-oh. Kings for the dealer."

Pardee bet his aces hard, and Slocum stayed in hoping to catch another king. Watley was struggling to fill his straight.

"You think Our Lordship's a little greedy?" Slocum asked Bassett.

"His enemies say he'd steal a red-hot stove."

"That what brought you over here anyway?" Slocum asked. "Filthy lucre?"

Slocum drew his third king, and Watley found the five. Slocum pushed a stack of double eagles across the baize. They raised and cross-raised until Slocum called.

Watley was betting hard on a busted straight.

"I'd like to say it was wealth, women, the love of adventure. Truth be known, I am not welcome in jolly old England."

"Sounds grim," Slocum said.

"Let us say that certain relatives persuaded me to seek my fortune elsewhere. Several thousand miles elsewhere."

"Must have been some persuasion," Slocum said.

"A lavish remittance if I left. Durance most vile if I stayed."

" 'Durance most vile'?" Slocum asked.

"There was a certain den of iniquity in London, not unlike this establishment, known as the Hellrake Club. Of course, its clientele is a bit more refined than the Rattlesnake's, but the activities are similar. I made the mistake of taking those activities to their outermost limits. You may not believe this, Mr. Slocum, but my personal nature is a violent one. I proved far too wild for my fellow Hellrakes, to say nothing of jolly old England."

"You got all that *dinero*, why are you in Mala Cruz?" Slocum asked.

"I'm here for the culture, the learned discourse, the intellectual stimulation."

"Really?" Bassett asked.

"I'm here for the money, you stupid cluck," Watley said. "At this very moment I'm investing in one of Díaz's mines, a little operation called La Fortaleza.''

"That's a slave labor mine," Slocum said.

"Indeed," Watley said, "and very cost effective. For years I'd wondered how Díaz managed it—to make so much profit on so little overhead. I tell you this new *El Presidente* has a genius for mining. Agriculture, too. At a time when it is so difficult to get good help, he is working labor-management wonders.''

Suddenly the door to one of the upstairs cribs flew open, and Captain Callahan was pushed out the door. He was buck naked, bound and gagged, his campaign hat on his head but his body covered with bloody whip marks.

Lady Hastings, still fully clothed, shot him five times with her .45. His body slammed into the balcony railing, cartwheeled over the top, and smashed their baize-covered poker table below.

"What's wrong, my dear?" said Watley.

"He was a shitty fuck," Her Ladyship said, strolling down the stairs.

Slocum glanced around the cantina. There was a big hardcase stranger up at the bar. He wore a black sombrero and matching poncho. He had a dark flowing mustache, and while Slocum couldn't see this face clearly, he looked like bad news.

There were also half a dozen Mexicans in crisscrossed bandoliers and sombreros, who seemed to have materialized out of nowhere. They glared at him with open hostility.

"Mr. Slocum, I should warn you I am not pleased with your actions this evening. I believe it was your lewd tongue that corrupted my niece and encouraged her to follow that nasty ruffian into his room. Furthermore, I believe you have systematically swindled my friends and me out of our rightful winnings. I, for one, will not tolerate a tinhorn.''

"You tell him, ducks," Lady Hastings said. She cocked

a leg on a chair and cracked a boot top with her quirt.

The Mexicans began fanning around the remnants of the poker table. Three of them, Slocum noticed, were armed with double-barreled Greeners.

"Well, Mr. Slocum," Watley said, "your sins have found you out. The trouble you have been searching for lies before you. Do you have any questions before we begin?"

Lady Hastings stood behind him. Bending down, she draped her bloody quirt around his neck and kissed him openly on the mouth.

Slocum pushed her away. "What's this? A lynching or a shotgun wedding?"

"It is what a great Spanish patriot, Frey Tomás de Torquemada, would have termed an *auto-da-fé*," Watley said.

There was no more table to play on, but still Slocum shuffled the cards.

"Game, anyone?" Slocum asked.

Watley convulsed with laughter.

It gave Slocum a moment to study the cantina. Overhead the whores were staring down on them. The tall slender one—the piano player—with the red stockings and garters and the long hair black as a raven's wing stared at him sadly.

Slocum thought, S'pose I'll never get a shot at you now. Or at the new one.

Suddenly, he spotted the new one, decked out in a long flowing black chemise and stockings, with matching hair and eyes—eyes hard and black as anthracite.

Belle Starr.

He glanced back at the bar and now recognized the hardcase gringo stranger—Frank James.

Aw, hell. Goddamn it to hell.

With elaborate precision, Slocum began dealing cards across the captain's bloody body.

"Cards," Slocum announced idly. "Queen on a red king. The trey's paired. Jack-high straight? No help to the lady."

Again, Watley rollicked with laughter.

As he dealt out the cards, Slocum reflected on his life. He remembered a girl named Poker Alice whom he had lived with for three months in Dodge. She'd had honey blond hair, fine bones, soft skin, and possessed a kindness and good humor that genuinely bewildered him. Looking back on their relationship, he wondered if he had loved her.

Perhaps. Still, Slocum could not help observing, three months had been a long time.

What *of* his life? A soldier, a wanderer, an outlaw, he'd spent four years making war and thirteen more on the owl-hoot. When he looked down his backtrail, he saw nothing more than women abandoned, horses shot out from under him and men killed.

He had so little to live for, he could not understand why he fought so hard to keep it.

He threw in his hand, then the rest of the deck.

"Dealer folds," he said to Watley.

"No kidding," the man answered.

Lady Hastings began massaging his neck.

"I think Mr. Slocum ought to be taught a lesson, a nasty lesson."

"A lesson in humility," Watley said. "Don't you agree, Mr. Slocum?"

"Why?"

"Because you're a dinosaur, something that should have been extinct fifty million years ago, something that belongs in a museum."

"You've outlived your time and your kind," Lady Hastings said.

"Because I took your money?" Slocum said.

"Precisely so," Watley said.

A pair of Mexicans brought the kitchen brazier into the cantina. They shoved a half-dozen knives into the hot coals.

Hot coals and knives. Jesus God, Slocum did not think he could stand extended torture.

"Yes," Lady Hastings said lightly, "I think that is exactly what our little boy needs, a nasty lesson in humility. I shall instruct. It's only fitting. Mr. Slocum, don't you agree?"

She cracked her quirt against a boot.

"Our lesson for today: Mr. Slocum, repeat after me. I am a lying cheat and deserve to be punished."

Slocum was silent.

"I said repeat after me!"

"Better repeat it," Pardee said. "It ain't nice to keep a lady waitin'."

Slocum said nothing.

"Mr. Slocum, you are acting like a very naughty boy." Her face was flushed with agitation. "Now repeat the words."

She brought the quirt down on the captain's body with a shattering *crack!*

Slocum looked his Lordship. "Watley, what is it you want?"

"Why, the money, ducks. It is mine, you know."

"Just between you and me, I won it."

"What's that got to do with old *numero uno?*"

"Rules of the game, Watley," Slocum said. "Winner takes all? Poker? It's what we were playing."

"We play by our own rules," Her Ladyship sniffed, "and the rules state most emphatically that *we win.*"

"There is no room for equivocation on that score," Watley said. "You beat us? Fine. You pay."

"The rules are relentless," Lady Hastings said.

"You pay most dearly," said Watley.

Pardee grinned. "Don't you just love watchin' a man get what's comin' to him?"

Slocum scooted his chair back against the adobe wall and counted the house. Bassett and Pardee were armed, naturally. However, Her Ladyship had not reloaded after shooting the captain, and Watley seemed to be weaponless. There were six *bandidos* gathering around the poker table, three of them with shotguns braced on hips. That was a bad sign indeed. There was Frank James, still up at the bar, stone faced, nursing a grudge. Who knew what Belle was plotting up on the balcony? Probably belting him with a spittoon.

"Well," Pardee grinned, "you don't look so cocky now. Got anything to say for yourself, Mr. Big Time Gunman?"

"Nothing at all."

"You're being modest, Mr. Slocum," Lady Hastings said. "I hear you're a very tough customer."

"No applause."

"I insist." She clapped loudly. "I like you tough. I want you to be the case-hardened, triple-distilled, blue-steel Wild West quintessence of toughness. Tough enough to whip Bill Sherman and U.S. Grant."

"I can't imagine why."

"Really?" Lady Hastings asked. "You don't know my motto?"

"I think I'm going to."

She pulled a heavy leather glove onto her right hand and slipped a seventeen-inch Bowie out of the brazier. Its smoking blade glowed red as the blazing coals.

"To every tough steak," Lady Hastings said, "comes a sharp knife. In your case a very hot sharp knife."

Bassett and Pardee grinned hugely.

Watley burst into applause. "Bravo! Bravo!" he yelled.

"Now, Mr. Slocum," Her Ladyship said, puckering her lips and blowing on the glowing blade, "you have been a very naughty boy. I want you to repeat after me. I am a lyin' cheat and deserve to be punished.''

Slocum said nothing.

Her Ladyship frowned and shook the smoking Bowie at him. ''Mr. Slocum, stoic silence will win you nothing. It will only make your ultimate fate—whining, whimpering, sniveling, begging—all the more humiliating.''

Slocum was silent.

''All right, Mr. Slocum,'' Her Ladyship said. ''If that is your final word, let's get on with it.''

She started back around the table toward him.

''This ought to be good,'' Bassett said, reaching for his gun.

''I seen lots of tough bulls in my life,'' Pardee grinned. ''No tough steers.''

Slocum shot Pardee through his grinning teeth. With his other Colt, he shot the Mexican nearest Bassett. The bandit's cocked shotgun discharged at a side angle, taking out a second Mexican.

Slocum was glad he'd learned to work a Colt with either hand. Bassett wore his holstered piece low on his thigh, and he was having trouble with his draw. When he finally got the gun out, he hurried his shot. The bullet hit high, blowing brown adobe dust all over the top of Slocum's head.

It had happened to Slocum before—at Shiloh and the panicky retreat at Vicksburg—that time had stopped for him. So it seemed now. To those at the table his hands were a blur, but to Slocum they were moving with ethereal slowness, the arms uncrossing, the cocked Colt in his right hand drifting toward Bassett, their eyes locking.

In this hair-trigger eternity—Slocum's arm extended, pistol leveled—Bassett's thumb groped for the hammer, and his lips mouthed mute curses, his gun helpless in his fist.

Slocum's Colt kicked. Blood blossomed in Bassett's chest, and his eyes flared.

A quarter of a heartbeat later, Slocum caught the blur of a Mexican's shotgun swinging up into his face. Without even bothering to aim, his left Colt shot out the man's right eye.

That was as far as he got.

Even as his right arm crossed over his left, he glimpsed the double shotgun barrels throwing down on him, the man's eyes squinting over the sights, the double hammers pulling back, his finger hooking around the twin triggers.

In that final heartbeat of forever, Slocum studied the man who was about to carve his scallop—his mahogany brown face, his flat obsidian eyes, his slavering lips curled over broken yellow teeth, the cartridge belts crisscrossing the front of his dirty muslin shirt.

The .56-caliber round from Frank James's Spencer hit the *bandido* in the back of the head, exiting through his right cheek in an explosive starburst of bone and blood.

Almost simultaneously with the Spencer's crash, Slocum heard overhead a shotgun's blast and saw the spread of its double-0 buck take out the pair of *bandidos* directly to his left.

He looked up to see Belle Starr, shrouded in a cloud of whitish shotgun smoke, the sawed-off six-gauge—barely visible—kicking high above her head, her face obscured by haze yet clearly smiling.

Time lurched, something clicked in Slocum's head, and his universe once again seethed with activity. Blood pumped, women screamed, bodies convulsed and settled. Belle was bounding down the stairs, her rebel yell— "YIP-YIP-YIP-YIP-YIIIIIP!!!"—ripping the night apart.

Frank James backed toward the door, his Spencer covering the room. His voice—a commanding presence—silenced everything and everyone.

"Nobody move! *Poco a poco, hombres*. Everything's gonna be just fine."

Nobody had the slightest intention of moving. Without even being asked, they had their hands up.

Belle—still in black chemise and stockings—collected the patrons' wallets, then shoved her Greener between the barkeep's eyes.

"Gimme that cashbox, *amigo. Mucho pronto*. 'Fore I blow your goddamned face off."

Slocum, meanwhile, collected the winnings scattered across Captain Callahan's body.

When he looked up, he saw that Watley and Her Ladyship were still directly across from him. Watley was still seated. Lady Hastings stood to his left, her right leg cocked on a chair, her lips sneering.

Watley's upper lip twitched uncontrollably, his eyes filled with rage.

Slocum shoved his bloody winnings into his money belt. Stepping over the captain's remains, he kicked Watley in the teeth, knocking him ass-over-teakettle.

"Bravo, Mr. Slocum, bravo!" Her Ladyship shouted. "I adore poise under pressure. You are truly *muy macho, un hombre duro*". A hard man.

Her sneer was magnificent.

The front sight of Slocum's Colt was filed razor sharp. When he brought the gun-barrel up alongside Her Ladyship's head, it cut her cheek to the bone.

"Let's move it out," Belle yelled to him.

Slocum stepped over Her Ladyship's prone body. Belle and Frank covered him while he shouldered his way through the batwing doors.

Part 7

We swore an oath. To Christ,
the Cause—to Quan*trill!*

—Frank James

49

Slocum squatted before their campfire. He rolled a quirly between his thumb and forefinger, licked it, then twisted both ends. He lit it with an ember.

He poured himself a cup of Arbuckle's coffee from the fire-blackened pot, then lay back against his saddle.

"Have a snort of this," Belle said. She tossed him a bottle of Jackson's Sour Mash from across the fire. "It'll get that coffee up on its feet."

He caught the bottle with one hand. "Looks familiar."

"It ought to," Kate said. "Liberated it from your room along with your Big Fifty."

He threw the coffee into the fire, then drank the whiskey from the bottle.

"Coffee a little strong?" Frank James asked.

"You could raise the *Merrimac* with it," Slocum said.

Doc leaned over next to Slocum and helped himself to a mess cup of sour mash.

"Ain't you offerin' the ladies a drink?" Kate Elder asked. "Seein' as how we saved the bottle."

"You mean I forgot to thank you?" Slocum said. He tossed her the bottle.

"All you done so far is snarl," said Kate.

153

"It ain't like you inconvenienced me or nothin'," Slocum said.

"Ain't you the grateful one," Belle said.

"Yeah," said Frank, "after the way we saved you from the hated foe."

"Wouldn't been no hated foe," Slocum said, "you hadn't stole my gold."

"You're a hard man, John," Kate said.

"Hard and unforgiving," said Belle.

"There's also one other time," Slocum said, "in Kansas? You shot me in the back and left me for rot."

"That's past prayin' for now," Frank said.

"Blood under the bridge," said Doc.

"My blood," said Slocum.

"Okay," Frank said, "you got a right to be pissed. I admit it. But you, Jess, and me, we rode a lot of miles together, killed a lot of men. We went through war and blood and heartbreak together. We were friends."

"Time-when," Slocum said.

"Nothin' changes what we went through," Frank said. "We were tempered in blood and fire. We came out steel."

"Time-when," Slocum repeated.

"Not for you and me. We was born together, died together." Frank pointed at him across the fire. "We went through hell together. Some things time don't change."

"Lawrence Town changed some things," Slocum said. "Them young'uns and old folks you killed, it changed *them*."

"We swore an oath," said Frank. "To Christ, the Cause—to Quan*trill!*"

"Quantrill." In Slocum's mouth the name was a curse.

"I heard you done for Quantrill yourself," Belle said. "In Lexington. Shot him down like a dog."

"Time-when," Slocum repeated.

"Time-*now*," Frank shouted. "That prison is *now*. My brother is *now*."

"You two settled that at Lawrence," Slocum said.

"Jess wasn't at Lawrence," Frank yelled.

"That wasn't very manly of him," Slocum said.

"It was Frank what held him back," Belle said. "He didn't want him to see it."

"But it was okay for the rest of us?" Slocum asked.

"Goddamn you," Frank shouted, "he was my little brother. I was supposed to look out for him."

"You done a great job," Slocum said.

"There weren't nothin' I could do," Frank said hoarsely. "It was like everything went sour. After you left, Red Legs attacked the farm. Hung our stepdad. Killed our kid brother. Ma lost an arm. They burnt the house and bullwhipped Jess halfway to death. Later, even after the war, there was no holdin' him back. Not after that. Not any of us."

Bob Ford, who'd been quiet all night, jumped to his feet.

"Goddamn you to hell, John Slocum," he shouted.

"Shut up," Frank James said.

"I ain't shuttin' up. We saved his ass in Mala Cruz, offered him a way to get his money back, and all he does is insult us. I ain't takin' it."

"I said shut up," Frank said.

"And I'm sayin' we could *make* him throw in with us," Ford said, slipping the rawhide thong off his Colt. "*I* could make him."

"*Make* me?" Slocum said, shaking his head.

"Give us a chance," said Kate. "Listen to our plan. Just one more time. Let me explain it again."

"Okay, the plan," Slocum said. "Let me see if I have it straight. You get me arrested by *federales*. They send me to La Fortaleza. You bust me and Jess out of an armed fortress of a jail, a gen-u-wine hard-rock prison, and because some dumber'n-dirt Injun whore—the *Comandante*'s whore, no less—is on the inside, helpin' out.''

"It don't sound promisin'," Kate had to admit.

"Don't sound promisin'?" Slocum said. "How can it miss? Just point me toward that prison. I'm beggin' you. Send me now. Lock me up. Please."

Slocum stood. He picked up his borrowed saddle, his bedroll, and headed up-canyon.

"Where you goin', John?" Belle asked.

"To be by myself. The company's better."

"We ain't finished explainin' *the plan*," Belle said.

"You ain't heard all the details," Kate said.

"Wanna bet?" He disappeared into the darkness.

Bob Ford stood up. He tightened the buckle on his buscadero rig and tied down his holsters.

"Sit down," Frank James said.

"Not hardly," said Bob Ford. "He can't talk to us like we're dirt."

"I said sit down," Frank James said.

"No sir, I can't let this slide. I ain't built that way. I'll shoot him where he stands."

"That'll be the day," Holliday snorted.

"I'm gonna—"

"—get yourself killed," Belle said.

Ford's face flushed.

"You hold your water, boy," Kate Elder said.

"He's just a man," Ford said. "He can die. Same as us. Any of us."

"You think so," Belle Starr said.

"Time-when," Frank said, "you couldn't walk in the same sun as John Slocum."

"Still can't," Kate Elder said, fixing Ford with a hard stare.

"He can still die," Ford said.

"Don't you understand?" Belle said. "You leave this firelight, he'll drop you like a dog. Like he was kickin' a tin can."

"And it won't mean squat," Kate Elder said.

"Just like he dropped those six men in Tucson," Frank said.

"And sixty more back in Clay and Jackson counties," said Belle.

"He messes with me," Bob Ford snorted, "he's just another asshole 'bout to die."

Belle started laughing. "You think to hole J. C. Slocum. What a hoot!"

"You think I ain't man enough?" Ford asked.

"You ain't man enough to shine his boots," Kate Elder said.

"Ain't you figured it out?" Belle said. "John Slocum was the best."

"Better'n Jess?" said Ford.

"*And* Coleman Younger," Belle said.

"I don't care. I still ain't—"

Frank James froze him with a look. "I said shut up." He turned to Kate Elder. "Kate, you sure he'll go all the way? You trust him on this? Once he's in there?"

"He's straight as a die," Kate said.

"As a plumb bob," Belle agreed.

"Belle," Frank said. "I want you helpin' Kate on this one."

"You think I ain't woman enough?" Kate said, indignant.

"If pussy was bullets, Kate, you could kill France. But it ain't. And I ain't takin' no chances, not with Jess. I want this one boxed and tagged."

"You're still sayin' I can't handle him," Kate Elder said.

"You just keep your face in his lap," Frank said. "I

want him dizzy, his eyes swimming. I don't want him to hear or see straight, not until he's in that prison with Jess— and brings him back.''

"And we get our gold," Holliday said.

Holliday, who had been sipping on the Jackson's Sour Mash, tossed Belle the bottle. She caught it in midair. Belle got up and took Kate by the arm.

"Let's go, girl," Belle said. "Looks like we got our work cut out."

50

Belle and Kate found Slocum behind a wagon-size boulder, leaning back against his saddle. His black Stetson was low over his forehead, but a Navy Colt was near either hand. The desert gets cold at night, and he was wearing his black coat to ward off the chill. They sat down on either side of him.

"We brought you a drink," Kate said, offering him the bottle of sour mash.

"Sort of as a peace offering," said Belle.

Slocum snorted but accepted the bottle.

"I'm sorry the way things turned out," Kate said.

Slocum's eyes were derisive.

"He don't believe us," Belle noted.

"He's got cause," Kate admitted.

"John," Belle said, "we could swear eternal love."

"Now he knows we're shuckin'," said Kate.

"I love you, John," Belle mocked gently. "I truly do. Don't that sound sincere?"

Slocum took another drink. "Never happen, girl. That love shit don't exist."

"Cynicism'll kill," Kate said.

"Damn straight," Belle agreed, helping herself to a snort of sour mash.

"We all got to believe in something," Kate said, relieving Belle of the bottle.

Slocum took back the bottle. "I believe I'll have another drink."

"Doc don't believe love exists neither, John," Kate said. "He says there's only need."

"That's me," Slocum said. "A slave to need."

"There's also greed," Belle observed. "Some friends of ours suffer from it real bad."

"Doc practically dots his i's with dollar signs," Kate noted.

"Frank'd take the dimes off a dead man's eyes and put back nickels," said Belle.

"Jess'd suck blood from a bat," Kate said.

"How'd we end up in such august company?" Belle wondered.

"Didn't live right," Kate said.

"Yeah?" Belle said. "Well, we can fix that. We got a chance to do it up proper this time."

"You mean you got a plan," Slocum sneered.

"Yeah, but it takes a second man inside that prison," said Kate, "one who ain't turned mountain oyster, who hasn't lost his balls."

"There's others," Slocum said wearily.

"Frank's shot through the chest. Doc's coughin' up his lungs."

"That kid, Ford."

"I'm talkin' *real* men," Belle said. "Men what rode by the light of the moon with Quantrill and Bloody Bill."

"You got some hard bark on you, even thinkin' stuff like that. Them friends of yours have robbed me of eighty grand, shot me in the back, and now *you* want to lock me up in a hard-rock slave-labor prison."

"You got any other plans?" Kate asked.

"Cash in my chips. Drift north. Find another game. Always did fancy Montana. Pretty country up there. Elk thick as buffalo once was. Trout practically fish *you*."

"We could always drift around down here, John," Kate said. "Just us three."

"Who you tryin' to shuck?"

"Straight deal," Belle said.

"Down *here?*" Slocum's eyes were contemptuous.

"You don't like Mexico?" Kate asked.

"Girl, I don't like nothin's been *near* Mexico."

"Nothin'?" Kate asked.

"I hate *peones, frijoles, federales,* brothers who pimp their sisters, boys who carry razors. Yes, I hate Mexico."

"Maybe we could get Cole out of prison," Belle wondered. "He'd help us."

"Now there's an idea," Slocum said. "Cole is dumb enough to go for somethin' like this."

"You shouldn't talk 'bout Cole like that," Kate said. "Belle was married to him once. Had his kid."

"It's okay," Belle said, shaking her head. "Slocum's got a point. Cole was not only dumb, he was *mean.*"

"Coleman Younger I knew, he hated to use a horse hard or a woman easy," Kate admitted grudgingly.

"He was rough on you too?" Belle asked.

Kate rubbed her crotch, as if in pain. "Cole once told me there was a fine line between pleasure and pain."

"Belle don't see no line at all," Slocum said.

"Same go for Jess?" Kate asked Belle.

"I liked Jess fine," Belle said. "Everybody did. You did once."

She stared at Slocum hard.

"Maybe, but I ain't goin' to prison for him."

"Your eighty grand plus half of the rest," Kate said.

"What about Holliday and the kid? What do they get?"

"Our undyin' gratitude," Belle said.

"You ain't a pair to inspire confidence."

"I wouldn't lie to you, John," Kate said.

"Me neither," Belle said. "Not ever."

"Jess said you were the best man he ever knew," said Kate. "Frank too."

"They never knew Hickok," Slocum said.

"You and Jess go back a long ways," Belle said.

"We rode the river," Slocum acknowledged.

"You'd be a team in La Fortaleza too," Kate said.

"Like nitro and glycerin," said Belle.

"What about that 'Pache *puta?*" Slocum mocked. "The one shackin' up with *El Comandante?* She's supposed to be our ace in the hole."

"She'll hold up her end," said Kate.

"Why don't I believe you?" Slocum asked.

Behind his back, Belle topped off Slocum's bottle with some Lydia Pinkham's. The tonic was spiked with tincture of opium. She scooted around and handed it to him.

"It's the last of the sour mash, John," Belle said. "You have it."

"I've had enough."

She poured in another slug of Lydia Pinkham's. She hoped he couldn't taste the opium.

"You'll never have a hangover," Kate said.

"Straight tongue?" Slocum asked.

"Gospel," Belle said.

He tossed it off.

"Damn, that tonic's bitter," he said, wiping his mouth.

"But good for what ails you," said Kate.

"I ain't got no female complaints," Slocum said, "outside of two particular whores."

"You just forgot how to take sides, John," Belle said.

"Too many years now you've stood outside it all. You got to get back in."

"There's a town over that *mal país* rise called Santa Madre," Slocum said. "What I'm gonna do is get my gear and stroll on down there. Get me a room and a whore."

"That's a two-mile walk, John," Kate said seriously. "This here's Apache country. I wouldn't chance it."

"And what you said 'bout that room and that whore," Belle said. "You don't need that. You got us and the stars."

"Time-when," Slocum said.

"That ain't hardly considerate," Kate said, "seein' how much we meant to each other."

Slocum felt very drunk. And very horny. He knew he ought to go, shake this crazy bunch just as fast as he knew how, but now he was aroused.

And the two women in front of him were desirable. There was no question about that.

Belle took him in her arms and kissed him openmouthed, her tongue rimming his gums, teasing his teeth, then darting in and out of his mouth in a perfect simulacrum of intercourse. He felt hornier than he'd ever felt in his life.

His head wanted to leave. His body wanted to stay.

Then Kate began undoing his belt, unbuttoning his fly.

"Whoa, girl," Slocum whispered, "I didn't say nothin' 'bout this."

"Just stay the night," Belle whispered hoarsely. "It'll work out all right. I swear."

Kate was now groping the immensity of his member. "I swear before God. I'll never do you wrong."

"I'll love you like the Good Book," Belle said, licking the inside of his ear.

"I'd be beholden," Kate begged, her voice an urgent rasp.

An abrupt wash of moonlight broke from behind the night

clouds, and Slocum could see, up-canyon, a dozen Apaches. They stood ramrod straight, motionless as stone, decked out in buckskin breechclouts and thigh-high rawhide-soled moccasins. Their necks were festooned with Navaho jewelry of hammered silver, leather bags filled with sacred objects such as owl feathers and lightning-blasted wood. Two braves sported vests over bare chests. Another favored a red flannel shirt, faded and torn at the elbows. Several wore army tunics with the sleeves and buttons cut off. For head gear they wore wore everything from forage caps to campaign hats, from Stetsons to stovepipes, from bowlers to beaded leather headbands.

Most of their clothes Slocum took to be raiding-party plunder.

When he reached for his Colt, Belle grabbed his wrist.

"Remember we told you 'bout *El Comandante*'s whore?" Kate said. She pointed to the one in the campaign hat. "That's Gokhlayeh, her husband."

"Gokhlayeh?" Slocum asked. "You mean Geronimo?"

"Him and his men are gonna help bust you boys out," said Belle.

"You, Jess, and Geronimo's bride-to-be," Kate said.

"Her name's Conchita," said Belle.

"They got Cohorn mortars, Hotchkiss mountain guns," Belle said. "Doc's pickin' up a crate of dynamite. We're settin' up a diversion for you three that'll make Shiloh look like Sunday-go-to-meetin'."

"Case you don't know," Slocum said, "our country's at war with Geronimo and his friends."

Slocum picked up his Winchester and his Sharps traveling case. He started off cross-country toward Santa Madre.

"John," Kate yelled, "you can't leave now. You ain't heard the rest of the plan. We're just gettin' to the good part. John? John?"

"John," Belle shouted, "you get back here. Frank, them 'Paches there, Kate, and me, we got a lot ridin' on this."

Slocum was now halfway up the *mal país* rise. He turned and faced the women one last time.

"Fuck Frank, fuck the Apaches, and fuck you," he said. Then he was up the slope, over the rise, and gone.

Part 8

A fool there was and he made his prayer,
Even as you or I . . .

—Rudyard Kipling, ''The Vampire''

51

Coming through the cantina door, John Slocum went straight for the bar. He needed a drink. It had been a short trek to Santa Madre, but his neck ached from staring down his backtrail.

Truth be known, he was still looking for those damn Apaches.

And he was mad. He felt as if he had a fist in his chest instead of a heart, and he was looking for a face to punch.

He paused to study the cantina. A single sprawling *sala* with a twenty-foot ceiling, thick overhead beams, and a massive balcony supported by huge alabaster columns. Its high walls were sparklingly white, gessoed to a brilliant sheen with the powdered gypsum deposited around the nearby rivers. Dozens of round tables, surrounded by quartets of bentwood chairs, were filled with scores of Mexicans in full *charro* regalia—elaborately embroidered sombreros, white muslin shirts crisscrossed with bandoliers, black pants tapered around the calf. Those seated smoked black cigars, bought drinks for the endless *putas* drifting from table to table, and played intense hands of poker and faro. Two to three men stood beside their *putas* in front of each of the curtained-off boltholes, waiting their chance at the painted doxies. Overhead, eight brass chandeliers, surmounted by conical tops of white damask, spread great circles of light around the room, most of it focused on the gaming tables. The light from the chandeliers' guttering candles jumped and flickered. The rest of the room was illuminated by coal oil lamps bracketed against the adobe walls.

The draped-off boltholes were kept deliberately dark.

Slocum found a place at the crowded bar and squeezed in. "Mescal," he said to the barkeep. "Leave the bottle."

He turned to study the upstairs balcony. That was where the expensive rooms were. He noticed one of the doors was wide open, and several of the upstairs women were leaning over the balcony, looking for business.

Slocum headed for the balcony steps. He still had his bloodstained winnings from Mala Cruz.

52

As soon as Slocum and his whore entered their room, Belle and Kate started up the steps. They knocked on the door of the big corner suite.

The door swung open, and they were met by a towering mountain of a man. He had a bullet-shaped head, shaved bald as a tangerine, and a black flowing mustache. His squinty eyes were blood streaked, and his blotchy cheeks, lined with broken veins, were slashed bone-deep by saber scars.

He wore tight black trousers tucked into matching hobnail boots burnished to a mirror gloss. Naked from the waist up, he wore a double-action Mauser in a shoulder rig. He had a massive chest and unnaturally long arms. He casually cracked his thigh with a riding crop.

"*Acht so!*" he roared. "*Bitte!* Two more *Dirnen, nicht wahr?*" Two more whores, yes?

"Not this time, Kaupfmann," Kate said.

"Some real interestin' business though," said Belle.

"More interesting than *hierher?*" Over here?

Still grinning, he stepped aside, offering them a view of the Presidente Suite. A vast chamber with a pair of broad bay windows, the room was dominated by a mahogany drawing table and chairs. In the back was a double-size canopied bed. Under its lavender sheets a *gringa puta* with lustrous hair whimpered into a pillow.

Near the bay window in a double-size brass tub bathed a stocky Mexican. His face was nut brown. Under his drooping mustache gleamed white teeth. Even in the bathtub he wore a *generalissimo*'s campaign jacket, heavily weighted down with medals. Many of them, Kate noted, were French.

Around the bathtub were scattered a dozen magnums of Dom Perignon. Kate suddenly realized he was bathing in champagne.

The man was none other than *El Presidente*, Porfirio Díaz.

The dripping head of a black-haired *mejicana puta* broke the surface.

"She is diving for sunken treasure, *ja?*" The German roared at his own joke.

"Even so," Kate said, "we got something you'll be interested in."

"Yeah," Belle said, "there's a fellow down the hall you'll want to meet."

"Nicht wahr?" Really?

"A *primo* candidate for La Fortaleza," said Kate. "A notorious desperado."

"You bother our *Excelencia* with this?" *El Comandante* frowned.

"He's also a world-class boxer," Kate said quickly. "The official champion of the Second, Third, and Seventh U.S. Armies."

"And *un hombre malo*," an evil man, said Belle. "He needs to be locked up real bad."

"Bravo!" Díaz shouted from his tub. He shoved the *puta*'s dripping head back under the champagne, and this time held it there. *"Muy bien*, we shall have ourselves a sporting contest. Tomorrow evening? *Verdad?"*

"Es verdad," El Comandante said, once again grinning.

The door to the rear room opened, and to Kate's surprise out stepped Lord Watley in his white duck pants, matching shirt, and Planter's hat. His cigarette holder was fixed firmly in his teeth. Pointing at the legal papers in his hand, he shouted:

"Don Porfirio, I am most pleased to now be co-owner of your mining operation. LA FOR-TAL-EZ-A!" Watley roared. "The name rings in my head like a bell! I tell you, *Excelencia*, we shall make a fortune. With your labor-management expertise and my financial contacts, we'll reap billions."

"The papers are signed?" Don Porfirio asked.

"Locked and cocked," Lord Watley thundered, "sealed and delivered." He handed the papers over to *El Comandante,* who, looking them over, nodded to Díaz.

The man's bathtub was now covered with air bubbles, so he released the *puta*'s head. She came up gagging and gasping, champagne streaming from her nostrils and mouth.

"Muy bien," Díaz said, patting her on the head. "Señor Watley, we have even better news this very evening. These two señoritas have located *uno desperado muy malo* down the hall, who is also *uno* prizefighter *muy famoso*. We shall have some fun tomorrow night around the ring, no? We have a new opponent for *El Comandante.*"

"Magnífico!" Watley shouted.

Three uniformed bodyguards appeared in the doorway of the second room.

"Two rooms down," El Comandante said, *"uno desperado muy malo*. We must be *muy* careful."

They stiffened to attention. *"Sí, Comandante,"* they shouted.

"Can Her Ladyship and I watch?" Watley asked. "It

might be interesting watching your men apprehend a true desperado.''

''Natürlich,'' El Comandante said. ''Your Ladyship, *macht schnell!''* Hurry. He threw the lavender sheet off her.

Lady Hastings was naked on the big bed, her wrists and ankles tied to the four posts, spread-eagled like a star. Her mouth was gagged, and she still whimpered.

Her rump, elevated by a pile of pillows, was covered with crimson stripes.

''Macht schnell!'' El Comandante shouted again, and cracked her scarlet bottom with his crop.

''He said hurry up.'' With wearing disdain, Watley threw her her nightgown, then cut her ropes. ''And do get a move on, old girl. Our new business partner has promised us a bit of fun. By the way, what is this desperado's name?'' he asked the girls.

But Belle and Kate were already heading back down the steps, pretending not to hear.

53

Slocum felt a light, eerie breeze across the back of his neck, but dismissed it as nerves. And maybe too much to drink. Truth was, all that booze had gotten him drunk.

This was unusual. Slocum did not get inebriated anymore. He'd lived too many decades on the razor's edge and the hair-trigger's touch to let down his guard. If nothing else, a lifetime of war, prison, and the owlhoot had taught him that much. Dropping your guard always cost you something.

Yet now for the first time in years, he didn't care. He was strangely relaxed—a sensation he'd been previously unfamiliar with—and it was not entirely unpleasant. Furthermore, he'd paid cash money for a whore—good money, goddamn it!—and for once in his life, nothing—absolutely *nothing!*—was going to distract him.

His second orgasm even failed to slow him down. A single adjustment for stride and rhythm, and he kept right on going.

"Ey, gringo, you don't never get enough, no?" his whore rasped.

"Honey," Slocum said, "ain't nothing down there 'cept blue twisted steel."

"Ey, amigo," she groaned, "you are indeed *muy hombre.*" Much man. "A compliment on your *machismo!*"

Her moaning sobs filled the room.

Slocum put his back into it, gave her everything he had. In fact, halfway into his power stroke, he decided to stretch it out—to bring her along with him, to time her own powerful climax to his.

He did not even hear the barefooted man open the door or slip across the room or the swing of his sap or the crack on his own skull.

All Slocum knew was that he was falling, falling, falling into the darkest deepest well in the world. For a while there was a pinpoint of light at the bottom, but then even that was gone.

After which there was nothing—just Slocum, the dark, and the void.

When he hit bottom, he knew no more.

Part 9

Born in this jailhouse
Raised doin' time.
Yes, born in this jailhouse
Near the end of the line.

—Malcolm Braly,
On The Yard

54

Dawn in La Fortaleza.

A slave-labor prison mine in the desert foothills of the Santa Madres, it is known throughout Sonora and Chihuahua provinces as hell on earth. In fact, there is a saying in Mexico. "Hell in Mejico is not in the hereafter but in the Fortaleza's pits."

The mining operations center on two hard-rock mountains—Monte de Muerte and Monte de Dolor. Mined first by the Mayans, then the Aztecs, then the Spaniards, and finally by a host of Mexican despots, their operations have always had one thing in common:

Slave labor.

Even the slave quarters remain the same. A dozen tiers of cells housing two thousand prisoners, carved out of a hard-rock cliff connecting the two mountains.

Surrounding these prison cells is a vast wall. Eighteen feet high, eight feet across, it is built of thick adobe blocks whitewashed to a brilliant alabaster. It has no gate and can be entered only through a deep passageway tunneling partly through and partly under the fortification. It is sealed at both ends by reinforced doors and massive crossbars.

The purpose of such extreme security is not to keep the prisoners in as much as the neighboring Indians out.

Land of the Apache, their rule is sustained by fear. What can be said of men who stake you out on anthills, face to the sun, then drip honey over your eyes and genitals? Who skin their victims to the bone? Who hang them from the heels over slow-burning fires? Who feed them their genitals while they're still alive?

Nor is the terrain friendly. Incomprehensibly ancient, the great Sonoran canyonlands stretch in all directions for hundreds of miles. Carved by long-vanished rivers into a vast labyrinth of crimson arroyos, these waterless chasms are arid as brick, hotter than hell's abyss.

Escape from La Fortaleza is not a viable possibility.

The processing of the ore has changed over the years. Transported by wheelbarrow and burden basket to the quarry, the ore is first crushed by sledgehammer-swinging convicts. These fist-size rocks are then hauled to the stamping mill, where they are smashed in water under quarter-ton *arrastras,* or stamps. The resultant sludge is shoveled over fine screens into slanted wooden troughs with slatlike riffles nailed across the rocker top. The worthless powder is sluiced down and washed out of the slanted trough. The heavy gold-bearing sediment, trapped behind the riffles, is scraped out for placer-stream refinement.

In the meantime miners die.

Life expectancy in the pits is measured in weeks.

If nothing else, the sheer heat of the pits will kill them, for the subterranean fires that thrust up these hills bake the tunnels like a hell-furnace. For every hundred feet of descent, the air temperature rises eight degrees, until at two thousand feet water does not drip from the facings but hisses and pops.

Mine fire is the greatest fear. The tunnels reek of dust and methane, oil and shale, and conflagrations howl through the mines. Igniting the timberwork, sucking out the air, they are constantly collapsing the shafts.

Nor is it much healthier on the pile. Swinging a sixteen-pound sledgehammer in a heat-choked, dust-haunted inferno eighteen hours a day is hardly salutary work. And for those whose hammers flag, there is the prospect of reduced rations, the guards' clubs, sweatboxes, flogging posts.

And death in the pits.

Some men, however, survive here.

Not long, but for a time.

Their hammers sing out, the echoing clang of steel and rock ringing across the pile.

The Fortaleza quarry.

Dawn in La Fortaleza.

55

A dark-haired man in striped convict pants hammered rocks on the rim of the La Fortaleza pile. Stripped to the waist, he had heavy shoulders, a thick neck, and the broad chest of a yearling steer. But even with his massive strength, his muscles burned, his back throbbed, and arms trembled.

That he'd once taken pleasure in weight lifting he now found amazing.

Nor was he pleasant to look at. He carried seventeen bullet holes: several in his chest and legs—two of them still a gaudy crimson—as well as under his pants, a slick, white starburst scar on his groin. He still bore the marks of a long-ago Jayhawker bullwhipping on his back.

This was a man not unfamiliar with violence.

He paused to study the quarry below. The sloping pile was four hundred yards across and almost as deep. It was filled with granite slabs and boulders on which he and the other three hundred prisoners hammered their ore. The men, most of them scrawny *peones* worked without pause. Three hundred hammers rose and fell, rose and fell, and the quarry reverberated with the ringing steel.

The three dozen gun bulls, in tan army uniforms, patroled the rim, seldom honoring the prisoners below with more than a glance. Their primary worry lay *out there*. This was the Land of the Apache, and the pile was four long miles from La Fortaleza's walls.

The hostiles had struck before with devastating effect.

Mostly, as Mr. Howard swung his hammer, he watched the trustees. These were ex-prisoners dressed in old ragged army uniforms, left over from the American Civil War. They roamed the quarry slopes, using axe handles as walking staves, shouting obscenities.

When production was down, they axe-handled the men.

It was a hard life, but Mr. Howard was not without hope. As captain of the prisoners' boxing team, he received extra rations, an occasional bottle of mescal, sometimes even one of the Fortaleza whores.

He also had friends on the outside, who hoped to spring him. Today, in fact, as Mr. Howard had stood role call in the big yard, the man who was to break him out had entered the prison right before his eyes.

Granted, he had not been an inspiring sight. The man was shackled to the floor of a prisoners' wagon and had been badly beaten. This was not a good sign, because, among other things, the escape plan depended on the new convict's physical strength.

Still the man on the quarry rim was not chagrined. He'd always walked the razor's edge. Even now, in his home state of Missouri, the governor was offering a fifty-thousand-dollar reward for his head.

What was the difference? he wondered. To die in the pits or be hanged by the neck from a Missouri gallows?

At least in La Fortaleza no one knew his real name.

So his hammer rose and fell, rose and fell; and while his muscles throbbed, his head was filled with dreams and schemes.

Mostly his thoughts centered on the man shackled to the prisoners' wagon. He wondered what had happened to him. Whatever it was, he hoped the man was all right.

He hoped to God he was all right.

56

A bucket of water hit John Slocum in the face.

When he came to, he found himself hanging from his bound wrists. The rope was made of thick hemp, and he swung from an overhead beam. His body felt as if it had been run over by a freight wagon. His ribs felt as if the twelve-span mule team had stomped him too.

Slowly, Slocum's vision cleared. He found he was eyeball to eyeball with Lord Watley. When his hearing returned, Watley was saying:

"You're a hard man, Mr. Slocum. You murder my associates, kick me in the face, pistol-whip Her Ladyship, and yet you show no remorse."

Now Lady Hastings approached. She was again decked out in black trousers and a shirt of red ruffled silk, open to the navel. Both were worn tantalizingly tight. Under her black scoop-brimmed Stetson, Slocum saw a long scar traversing her right cheek—a red mean bitch of a scar. Her eyes blazed.

"I think the man's out of touch with his feelings," she said.

"*Garçon,*" Watley said to the guard, "put Mr. Slocum back in touch with his feelings."

A large-framed Mexican guard, in jackboots and a tan

federale uniform, slipped on a pair of heavy canvas gloves.

"Please, *garçon*," Lady Hastings said, "take your coat off. It's a warm day."

"Indeed," Lord Watley said, "we do want you comfortable."

The man slipped off his coat. Measuring Slocum for a straight right, he hit him in the stomach as hard as he knew how. Circling, he then worked on him as a boxer might work on the heavy bag. He hit the kidneys and chest with hard rights, then hammered the stomach and groin with left hooks and uppercuts. When one of the blows mercifully caught Slocum under the heart, he passed out.

Another bucket of water, and he came to. Once more, he heard His Lordship's voice, distant and tinny, as if from the far end of a tunnel.

"I say, what makes Mr. Slocum so tough?"

"My presence. Being a woman, he expects me to show him mercy."

Watley burst into laughter.

"What's so funny?" Lady Hastings asked.

"The thought of it! Someone expecting mercy from *you*."

She gave Watley a superior smile. "Yes, it is rather amusing, I suppose."

"Quite."

Through blood-streaked eyes, Slocum studied the room. He appeared to be in a dungeon of sorts. The black blood-stained walls were lined with manacles and knives. In one dark corner Slocum saw an iron maiden and in another a rack. Bullwhips, quirts, and cat-o'-nines hung from the overhead crossbeams.

"I say, you aren't foolish enough to expect mercy from me, are you?" Lady Hastings grabbed Slocum by his sweat-soaked hair. "My heart is a veritable tomb of blue ice."

"You do seem pissed," Slocum rasped.

"Well, *what* do you expect?" she asked, indignant.

"You mean 'cause I hit you?"

"There were other things too," she said.

"It was only a card game," Slocum said.

"You miss the point, *Dear Heart*."

On *Dear Heart* she cracked a boot top with her quirt.

"What point?" Slocum asked hoarsely.

"You did not let me *win!*" Watley roared.

The guard went back to work on Slocum. Again, he passed out. Again, the guard hit him with water.

To Slocum's dismay, he came to.

"Ummmm," Her Ladyship said, poking Slocum's bruises with the butt stock of her quirt, "that must really smart."

Slocum winced at her touch.

"Yes, they bloody well do," Lord Hastings said. "Still, this is the way I like you ruddy Yanks, hung like meat, bleating for the shears, ripe for the slaughter."

"That the way you see Díaz?" Slocum asked.

"Oh, not at all," Watley said. "I look on him as a lost brother, a secret sharer. It's as if we were joined at the hip."

Slocum stared at him.

"He and I do think alike, you know," Watley said. "Why, just look at the way he's organized La Fortaleza here—his ingenious exploitation of the mineral resources, his efficient labor-management techniques. He can persuade his peons to do virtually anything."

"And without a single syllable of complaint," Lady Hastings observed.

"Quite a bit different from their counterparts in Europe and the United States," Watley said.

"No union problems here!" Her Ladyship sang out.

"Well said. I can't wait to introduce him to some of my backers on the Continent."

"He runs this place with slave labor," Slocum said through gritted teeth.

"And rightly so," Lady Hastings said. "His peons deserve no less."

"*Our* peons deserve no less," Lord Watley said. "After all, we *are* partners with him now."

"But slavery?" Slocum said.

"Oh dear," said Lady Hastings. She chucked Slocum's chin with mock pity. "I believe our friend suffers from bourgeois guilt."

"Middle-class morality," Watley said.

"He probably also feels sorry for all those darkies he fought to enslave," Lady Hastings said.

"You did fight for the South, old sport," Watley pointed out. "Remember?" He rapped one of Slocum's cracked ribs.

Again, Slocum winced.

"Oh my," Lady Hastings said, "I think we've hurt his feelings." Her upper lip curled at the word *feelings*.

Slocum looked away.

"We're losing him," said Lady Hastings.

"*Garçon!*" Watley said, summoning the guard. "Mr. Slocum requires further instruction."

"A refresher course in human anatomy should do the trick," Lady Hastings said.

Again, the beating.

Again, Slocum was revived.

Watley and Hastings were nose to nose with him.

"How *is* it hanging?" Watley asked.

"Not too good."

"What a bad break for you," Watley said.

"I believe," Lady Hastings said, "your luck has taken a turn for the worse."

"Indeed," Watley said, "you are about to undergo a stern rite of passage."

"I shall escort you through it personally," Lady Hastings said.

"Her Ladyship is quite thorough. You have my word."

"Trust me, Mr. Slocum, I shall touch you to the pit of your soul, to the bottomless well of that loathsome womb in which you were ostensibly born."

"Watley, what is it you want?" Slocum could barely get the words out.

"Instant gratification of my desires. It's not too much to ask."

"Of course, in Lord Watley's case," her Ladyship said, "his desires consist solely of greed, violence, and terror."

"Let us never overlook the value of terror," Watley said.

"Terror?" Slocum asked, confused.

"It's why we're in Mexico, ducks," Lady Hastings said. Taking a deep breath, Watley roared: "Isn't this a wonderful country?"

"I hate Mexico," Slocum said.

"W-h-a-a-a-t?" Watley was skeptical.

"*Muchachos, frijoles, federales,* I hate everything about Mexico."

"I hope that doesn't include my business partner, Don Porfirio?" Watley said.

Slocum nodded.

"Ummmmm," Lady Hastings said, "*El Presidente* won't be pleased to hear that."

"Too bad."

"Too bad for you," Watley said. "You see, Don Porfirio, Her Ladyship and I have been waiting for you a long time. Longer than you can ever imagine."

"Friend Slocum, you are now on the outermost rim of injustice. Blindness, castration, dismemberment, *death*—" She lingered lovingly over the word *death*. "—all these you shall sample in due course."

"One at a time," Watley said.

"You know, Dear Slocum," Lady Hastings said, "the worst thing about dying? It's so disgustingly common. Everybody does it. Stableboys, whores, kings, queens, the lowest gutter trash, Olympian gods. Perhaps even I shall one day shuffle off this mortal coil."

"But not before friend Slocum," Watley said.

"No, not before you, ducks." Lady Hastings chucked him under the chin again.

The door to the oubliette lifted, and the dark dungeon was flooded with light. *El Comandante* climbed down the steps. Kaupfmann was dressed in full Prussian drill, including saber and double-action Mauser, epaulets and slashed cuffs, jackboots and spiked helmet.

"I thought ve vould find you here," Kaupfmann said. He gasped when he looked at Slocum. *"Acht du lieber!* Ve must cut him down. *El Presidente* vill be furious if you hurt his hands. *Ah gut. Sie sind ausgezeignete."* They are excellent. "Herr Slocum, *El Presidente* will be in the front row tonight. Ve vill giff him a gut show, *nicht wahr?"*

Slocum had no idea what he was talking about.

El Comandante cut him down with his saber. The guard caught him under the arms.

"Ah, Herr Slocum," he said, patting Slocum's cheek, "can you imagine my surprise when I learned a fellow pugilist, a gentleman of the ring, would arrive in La Fortaleza? The Champion Boxer of the second, third, and seventh American Armies, no less."

Slocum could barely stand, and his back and stomach felt like they'd been stomped by a bull.

"You want Mr. Slocum to fight *tonight?*" Lady Hastings asked.

"*Naturlich, Fraulein Hastings,*" Kaupfmann said.

"I suppose," Lord Watley said, "we can always continue our own little *tête-à-tête* another time."

"But, of course, Herr Watley. You are the new co-owner of La Fortaleza."

"Splendid," Watley said.

"What do I get out of this?" Slocum asked.

"Food, drink, the next day off," Kaupfmann said. "And if you defeat me, you can spend the night with my own special *Madchen*, La Conchita." He whispered to Slocum. "She is virgin."

"It is his standing offer to all fighters," Watley explained.

An Indian girl came down the dungeon steps. She had a generous mouth, a strong chin, and black flashing eyes framed by flaring cheekbones. She was dressed in an elaborately beaded robe of spotlessly white buckskin. Her thigh-high rawhide-soled moccasins curled up at the toes.

The young bride of Geronimo.

La Conchita.

"You win, friend Slocum," Her Ladyship said, "you get a night of wonder and revelation."

"I believe the word's *fornication*," Watley said.

"Bravo! Bravo!" Díaz's booming laugh boomed through the oubliette. He descended the steps in his *generalissimo's* uniform, heavy with braid, garish with ribbons and medals. He was smoking a foul-smelling cigar and grinning. "She is *muy magnifica,* Senor Slocum, no? *Una india pura virga.*" Pure Indian virgin. "The most beautiful *puta* in *Mejico.*"

"To the victor belongs the spoils," Kaupfmann said.

"But such a prize does not come cheap," Díaz said. "*El*

Comandante is the *numero uno* fighter in both Mejico and Prussia. You must be at your best.''

Slocum could barely stand, but Díaz did not seem to notice.

"*El Comandante*," Díaz said, "I trust you will remove him from this room?''

"I will send him to *prisionero* Howard.''

"*Muy bien*," Díaz said. "He is *el capitán* of the *prisionero*'s boxing team. He will get you ready.''

As Slocum mounted the steps, his arms felt like they were made of lead.

57

The guard pointed to the quarry's south rim. With a sixteen-pound sledgehammer in his fists, he followed the guard toward it.

Halfway around the pile, standing beside a long flat granite slab, they found the man called Thomas Howard.

"I seen better-lookin' corpses," Jess said.

"It's hard bein' alive," Slocum acknowledged.

The sun was at zenith, and Slocum took off his striped convict's shirt. His upper body was a mass of livid bruises.

"You outdid yourself, boss," Jess said to the screw.

"Just see that he is *preparado*," said the guard.

The *guardia* mopped his forehead with a bandanna, took one last look at the scorching, dust-choked pile, and headed back to La Fortaleza.

Jesse put a chunk of hard-rock ore—the size of a mis-shapen watermelon—on the granite slab. He grabbed his sledge by its sweat-slick handle and, swinging it high overhead, hit the melon-size chunk as hard as he knew how. The *clang!* of steel on rock rang out clear and high, echoing across the quarry.

A small cloud of rock dust billowed above the ore chunk. Its surface did not register a dent.

Slocum lined up a dozen rocks of his own on the slab and broke them with effortless ease.

"I been waitin' for you, you know," Jess said, struggling with his rock.

"I don't want to know," Slocum said.

"The hell you don't," Jess said. "I'm the one what brought you here."

"Don't tell me."

"Thought the whole thing up myself."

Slocum stared at him.

"We're gonna make *mucho dinero*, boy," Jess said. "I not only got your gold all nice and safe, I got us a shot at Porfirio's stash."

"Ey, you two, pick it up." From down the quarry slope, a walking boss was yelling, shaking his axe handle at them. "*Muy pronto*, no?"

The two men resumed swinging.

"I'm tellin' you Díaz's got a thousand gold ingots buried under that mountain. I was just figurin' my plan of attack when those damn *federales* closed in. If they hadn't trapped me, I'd have gotten it all."

Just above the rise appeared an endless army of miners, heading back from the pits. Slocum nodded toward them.

"We get too weak for these hammers," Slocum said, "they send us down to the mines. Like them boys there. Life expectancy's less'n a month in the pits. They say the mine fires are worse than the rats and the poison gas. Any truth to that, Jess?"

"Now, John, don't go frettin' on that. I tell you we're comin' out of this millionaires."

The army of miners was circling around the quarry's rim. There looked to be a thousand of them. They were covered with dirt and dressed in rags. Hollow-cheeked and empty-eyed, they were nothing but skeletons with a little parchment stretched over them. They were all limping and bent over. They were close enough that Slocum could see their scrawny limbs and rotten teeth. Several had lost their hair and teeth both. Their backs were covered with whip marks, their bodies with scabrous, maggot-ridden sores. Slocum heard their dust-blackened lungs coughing up bloody phlegm.

"I got it worked out. I swear to you, John, we're gettin' out."

Slocum's eyes flared. He swung his hammer one-handed, and for a second Jess thought Slocum would brain him. Instead he nailed Jesse's ore chunk with a single devastating stroke.

His hammer's *clang!* was loud enough to draw stares.

The rock shattered like glass.

"We're gettin' out, huh?" Slocum said.

"Damn straight, partner," Jess said. "All you got to do is hammer *El Comandante* tonight like you done that rock, and we'll be over those walls like big-assed birds."

"Those walls got Gatling guns on them."

"Okay," Jess said. "You don't like my plan, you don't have to fight him."

"Yeah?"

"And tomorrow you can line up for the mines."

He had Slocum there.

Slocum placed more rocks on the slab. Again, he demolished them with speed and precision.

"Kaupfmann ain't no Sunday-Go-To-Meetin'," Slocum finally said.

"You can still whip him."

"You think so?" Slocum muttered.

"He's got a bad right side. Believe his liver's going. I discovered that when I was fightin' him."

"Did he go down?"

He placed Slocum's right arm alongside his own, fist to

shoulder. His own fist barely reached Slocum's biceps.

"I ain't got your height, weight, or reach." Jess said. "That fat Kraut hammered me to pieces."

"Wish I could've been there."

"You just slip his right and hook that side, you'll take him out," Jess said.

"My gut ain't no better," Slocum said, still tender from his beating. "You sure it's gotta be tonight?"

"These matches are the only time Kaupfmann empties out them cells."

"You're lookin' to free them prisoners too?"

"Just don't want to get them all killed," Jess said. "Under them cells Kaupfmann keeps a couple tons of Herculite."

"Blastin' powder?"

"Capped and primed on a short fuse. All Kaupfmann has to do is blow one keg, and sympathetic detonation blows the rest."

"Locked and cocked," said Slocum.

"Frank and them bronco bucks'll rip this jailhouse like howitzers. I don't want him murderin' fifteen hundred men when they get here."

"How's Frank gettin' over them walls?"

"We got a Trojan Horse."

"And all I got to do is whup this Kraut?"

"That and a few other things."

"What *else* you got planned for me?"

"You'll find out when you meet our Trojan Horse."

"Jess, what is *this*?"

"La Conchita'll tell you everything after the fight. From there on out, it's her show."

"Tell me what?"

"She's gonna have some weapons for you."

"What's this Injun whore up to?"

"Damn, you ask a lot of questions. Didn't Belle and Kate 'splain nothin' to you."

"'Splain what?"

"That we got a *plan*."

"I don't feel so good," Slocum said, rubbing his gut.

"I can fix that."

"I don't think so."

"Try some of this." Jess took a bottle of patent medicine out of his pants pocket. *"Lydia Pinkham's Special Elixer for All Female Complaints*. Good for what ails you."

Slocum's face turned white as a ghost.

For a moment he was sure he'd be sick.

58

Three men, in *federale* uniforms, squatted along the rim of the cliff. It was near dusk now, and time to get started.

Gokhlayeh—the one the white-eyes called Geronimo—disliked his uniform, especially the bloody holes in it. But otherwise he was content. He lashed his bag of climbing spikes to his belt and slung two crisscrossing coils of rope over his shoulders and chest. He was ready to lead the white-eyes across the cliff face.

It was a steep precipice, nearly a thousand feet straight down and three-quarters of a mile across, but Gokhlayeh was not concerned. He could tell from here that there were plenty of hand- and footholds to free-climb the face.

The spikes and ropes were for the white-eyes, not him.

Actually, Gokhlayeh was looking forward to the evening. A good climb across this cliff, then a shorter one up over the back wall of La Fortaleza, and the battle to liberate La Conchita would begin.

A good battle was just what he needed.

He'd been idle too long.

It was time he got out and killed somebody.

Almost as an afterthought, he wondered why the *pindahs* looked so scared.

59

As Jess led the way through the Fortaleza prison yard, Slocum could not believe what was happening to him. On all sides he was surrounded by *prisioneros*—nearly two thousand in all. Many of them were seated in the grandstands, but most were on foot, crowding around the ring for a better look. They were little more than scarecrows in striped uniforms, filthy, ragged, starving—yet nonetheless excited.

In the center of the throng, Slocum saw the roped-off boxing platform. He looked for canvas but there was none. Just a hardwood floor.

Getting knocked down would be a real treat.

Fighting his way through the mob, Slocum climbed up onto the platform and slipped under the ropes. Jess dragged his stool away from one of the fans, and Slocum sat down.

Dressed in a pair of cutoff *prisionero* pants and ankle-high moccasins, Slocum slipped his *sarape* off his shoulders.

Craning his neck, he studied the crowd. They had to be the worst spectators in the history of pugilism. To Slocum, the *prisioneros* didn't look like boxing fans at all, but a hungry mob of rabid dogs.

Now the crowd exploded with boos and insults.

"Fuego! Pegale al cojones! Cojones! Abajo!"

Jesse smeared neat's-foot oil along the bridge of Slocum's nose and around his eyes. He then began bandaging up his fists.

"Try not to break any knuckles on Kaupfmann's hard head," Jess advised.

Slocum glared at him, and Jess got mad.

"Goddamn it," Jess shouted in his ear, "don't be so negative. You can whup the man. I know it."

"You think so, huh?"

"Thinkin' don't get it done. It's *wantin'* it what counts. You got to *want* this man so bad you can smell it, hear it, breathe it. It's got to be in your blood, goddamn it. And you do *want* it. I know it. You gonna kick his ass so hard, he's gonna have to slit his throat to shit. You ain't just gonna whup his sorry ass, you gonna kill the sonofabitch."

"I am?"

"There you go with that negativity. You don't *want* it, you're gonna rot on that pile and die in those mines. Now do you *want* it?"

"I want it."

Slocum couldn't believe he was saying this.

"I said do you want it?"

"I said I want it."

My God, Slocum thought, he actually said it twice.

"I said do you want it?"

"I don't feel like sayin' it three times," he shouted.

Suddenly, he heard a tremendous roar. The mob parted, and *El Comandante,* draped in a purple satin robe and surrounded by a phalanx of armed guards, approached the boxing ring.

The crowd, to Slocum's dismay, gave their warden a thunderous ovation.

60

Díaz stood in front of the gilt-framed bathroom mirror, trimming his mustache. He had two gorgeous *putas gringas* waiting for him on the hacienda's veranda, and he wanted to look his best for them.

Putting down the scissors, he paused to examine his uniform. He was wearing a tan *generalissimo's* tunic with full cuffs and densely braided epaulets. His chest was covered with medals and ribbons, and on his hip he wore one of those newfangled double-action Mausers that his *Comandante* had recommended so highly. His large, square face was a little dark for his own tastes, but what the hell. His bushy mustache was sufficient proof of his Castilian blood.

He placed his plumed shako firmly on his head and returned to the drawing room. Looking at the two women on his fourth-story veranda, he decided these were the two most beautiful *putas gringas* he'd ever had. They sat out on the wicker settee—the raven-haired one dressed in a jet-black silk chemise and stockings, and her red-haired friend in a crimson corset and matching fishnet hosiery.

In front of them a magnum of Dom Perignon chilled in a silver ice bucket. Below, *El Comandante* was preparing for his boxing match with the new contender, prisionero Slocum.

Opening the French doors, he joined the two ladies.

"Ah, ladies," he said expansively, "a compliment on your patience. It is a true crime that as head of state I am take away from your exquisite company." He kissed their hands passionately. Kate plumped the settee cushions and pulled him down between them. Belle poured him another goblet of champagne.

"Hell, *Presidente*," Belle said, "a man of your *machismo* must get a lotta that there head of state."

"Must have *putas* stashed all over Mejico," said Kate.

"Some of them real hot, I bet," Belle said.

"But not as hot as my two *chiquitas*, no?" Díaz said.

"We're the hottest *chiquitas* this side of hell," Kate said, stroking the inside of his thigh.

But the Don was suddenly distracted.

"Here he comes," he shouted, *"El Comandante*. We must watch. His entrance will be *muy grande*. He is climbing into the ring even now."

"He really any good?" Kate asked.

Don Porfirio kissed the tips of his fingers. "He is truly *magnífico*."

"Think he can whip that gringo Slocum?" Belle wondered, pointing at their battered friend slumped on his stool.

"There is no one he cannot beat," Díaz said. "He is truly *el supremo*."

"You think so?" Kate was concerned now.

"Watch and listen," Díaz said.

61

El Comandante stood in the center of the ring. He lifted his right hand, and the hysterically cheering crowd hushed. He began haranguing the throng in heavily accented German-Spanish.

"What's he sayin'?" Slocum asked, confused by the dialect.

"Ain't nothin'," Jess said. "just a lot of braggin'."

"I asked, what's he sayin'?"

Jess was standing behind Slocum, trying to loosen him up, massaging his neck and shoulders.

"Well, he is gettin' a little rough right here," Jess admitted. "Says he's not gonna actually box you. Says he's gonna draw, quarter, and castrate you. Then he says he's gonna fry your *cojones* in some chili sauce and have them for breakfast. Says all us gringos are nothing but sons of whores and mountain oysters anyways. Says we aren't good enough to be doin' time with real men. When he's finished in the ring, recommends these *hombres* here should take you out back of the latrines and do you like a girl."

The crowd roared now.

"OLÉ! OLÉ! OLÉ! OLÉ! OLÉ! OLÉ!"

El Comandante raised his hands for silence, then continued his harangue.

"Well, go on," Slocum said impatiently. "Translate."

"Says, on the other hand, that may not be possible. When he's finished, he claims, there won't be enough left of you for the birds to carry away."

El Comandante threw off his purple satin robe and pointed at Slocum with an angry accusing finger. He followed with a torrent of pidgin Spanish.

"Go on," Slocum grunted.

"Says you're dead meat, dead already. Says you just don't know enough to lay down. Says it's time someone threw some dirt on you."

"Is he always so friendly-like?" Slocum asked.

"Got to admit he does seem riled."

"What's he sayin' now?"

"Says, '*Hay que tomar la muerta como si fuera amante.*' You've taken death as a lover. Says he sees death sittin' on your shoulder like a bird. Says, in fact, you're deader than dead, deader than the grave, dead as dead can be."

"Cheerful, ain't he?"

"Aw, hell. I didn't think he'd do this."

"What is it?"

"Turn around."

A half-dozen guards were setting up a pair of sawhorses just behind Slocum. They began spreading two-by-fours and four-by-eights across them.

El Comandante bounded down off the platform and strode up to the display.

The prison yard thundered with the roar of "*OLÉ!*"

With the edge of his hand, *El Comandante* shattered each of the pieces of lumber.

When they stacked them up two and three high, he shattered the piles, the end pieces sailing a dozen feet in the air.

Jess continued massaging Slocum's neck muscles.

"He's just tryin' to spook you," Jess said.

"He *is* spookin' me."

Next Kaupfmann shattered an oak log eight inches in diameter.

The crowd's roar was tumultuous.

"Just stay loose," Jess shouted in Slocum's ear. "That's nothin'. Logs can't hit back. You can."

Slocum averted his eyes.

The ovation now reached seismic proportions.

"Why they cheerin' so hard?" Slocum asked.

"*El Comandante* wins, they get a ration of mescal."

"Gather they ain't been disappointed yet."

"No," Jess said, "but they're gonna be in for a bitter disappointment toni—Aw, hell!"

Slocum wheeled around. Two guards were leading a black range bull up to the boxing platform by its nose ring.

"What is *that?*" Slocum asked.

"Some of *El Comandante's vaqueros* caught him out in the mesquite. Kept him out back for sport, they said. Should have guessed this would be the sport. Díaz loves this one." Jess grinned enthusiastically despite himself. "Got to admit the old *Comandante* puts on a real good show, don't he?"

Kaupfmann raised his hands, hushing the audience.

For one heartbeat of eternity there was stunned silence.

El Comandante wheeled around and hit the bull off the pivot, squarely between the eyes.

The big bull dropped to his knees as if he'd been shot, not slugged.

The crowd was beside itself, their "*OLÉ!*'s" reverberating over the yard like thunder.

Hopping back up onto the platform, *El Comandante* ducked through the ropes and reentered the ring.

He gave Slocum a grin.

Slocum felt his heart sink.

62

Lady Hastings and Lord Watley stood in the veranda doors and watched *El Comandante* duck back into the ring. Watley joined in the crowd's applause, while Her Ladyship cracked her boot tops with her quirt.

When the applause died down, Lady Hastings gave Díaz a polite smile, then joined them on the settee.

"So nice of you to invite us up here, Don Porfirio," she said. "Lovely seats, if I do say so."

"I must say, I do admire that man of yours," Watley said, taking a seat beside Her Ladyship. "He does get things done."

"Just one little thing, however, if I may ask?" Lady Hastings said.

"But of course," Don Porfirio said. "Whatever you wish."

"We only hope there is something left of Mr. Slocum when your man finishes with him," Lady Hastings said. "Lord Watley and I had certain plans for Señor Slocum."

"Grave plans," Watley said.

"My *Comandante* is totally cognizant of your desires," Díaz said. "We were quite clear on that count."

"How can we ever thank you?" Lord Watley said.

"Por favor," Díaz said. "It is nothing. The gringo is yours."

"Splendid," Watley said.

"Marvelous." Then Lady Hastings muttered to Watley under her breath, "I can't wait to get my tingling talons into that one."

63

Another spectator stared at the proceedings.

Geronimo, still attired in his *federale* uniform, peered around the edge of the cliff face, and observed the events in the big yard below.

He was bewildered. For many-seasons-past the chief had watched the *pindah-lickoyee*—the white-eyes—rape the land, exterminate its beasts, violate the bellies of the sacred mountains, tunnel through the earth like moles, and lock his people up in places like La Fortaleza in their *pindah* quest for the worthless yellow metal.

Geronimo had never had any doubts. He knew the white-eyes were fools.

And the events of the evening suggested it was worse than that. That the men below would bruise their fists hitting boards and bulls—all apparently for the delight of their filthy, ragged slaves—was more than folly. It was insane.

He glanced over his shoulder at the two pindahs behind him. One of them was truly ill. The one they called Doc kept coughing blood into rags.

Geronimo had wanted to pitch him over the side of the cliff, but the one called Frank would not allow it. He had drawn his gun and threatened to shoot Geronimo if he tried. The one called Frank preferred that his friend die slowly, agonizingly, bleeding from the lungs—and maybe get them all killed.

Some friend.

Not that Frank was of any use. He was terrified of the cliff and climbed even more slowly than the sick one. Right now both of them cringed on a ledge, a few feet behind him.

Doc coughing up blood.

Frank mumbling over and over: "I can't stand heights! I can't stand heights!"

If he couldn't stand heights, why did he climb the cliff?

None of this made any sense to Geronimo. Not the behavior of the Mexican pigs below. Not the behavior of the white-eyed pigs to his rear.

So be it. He would free his bride-to-be himself. He would attack the Gatling gun tower by himself. He would show these white-eyes what a real man is made of.

For one thing, the sentries on the wall were all preoccupied. They stared at the men in the ring, laughing, drinking, pointing, making lurid jokes about each other's mothers, fathers, and sisters.

He would never understand the *pindah-lickoyee* or their half brothers, the *mejicano* scum.

Never.

Trying to walk like a *mejicano* pig, Geronimo left the two *pindahs* on the cliff and strode off along the broad wall top toward the nearby gun tower.

64

Jess was explaining the rules to Slocum:

"They're real simple. You fight till one of you gets knocked out. You're then dragged off to your stool, where your trainer revives you."

"How do you decide who won?"

"The winner's declared when one of you can't be revived."

Slocum's eyes were bleak.

"Now don't even think like that," Jess said. "You think how bad you want to sail over them walls. Think of that 'Pache *puta* you'll be beddin' down. Think of all that tequila you'll be drinkin'. Think of kickin' *El Comandante*'s ass all over this sorry excuse for a boxin' ring."

Slocum put his head between his legs.

Now *El Comandante*—dressed in black circus tights with matching high-tops and leather gloves—was prancing and shadow boxing around the ring. If he looked big before, he now looked prodigious.

Ortero—their overweight captain of the guard—doubled tonight as referee. He looked miserable. It was hot in the ring, and his face was streaming with sweat, his shirt soaked through.

But finally he hammered the ringside bell.

Slocum came out of his corner and moved toward the *Comandante* carefully. Kaupfmann's big barrel chest rippled with muscles, and he radiated cockiness. As he moved toward Slocum, he muttered German obscenities:

"Schweinhund! Scheisskopf!"

Oddly enough, the man's arrogance had a salutary effect on Slocum. It was as if for the first time since coming to La Fortaleza he recognized the real enemy. This swine swearing at him was the one out to get him.

It energized Slocum. Moving in, he stung *El Comandante* with two long jabs. He stepped in again, jabbing him once more, then hooked him hard in the mouth, drawing blood.

El Comandante had not been hit like that in ages—and never by a *prisionero*. He'd never had a convict bold enough to loosen his teeth, bloody his mouth, and puff up an eye. His convicts all knew the consequences of provoking his wrath—the torture chamber, the flogging post, the sweatbox, the endless weeks on starvation rations. It was easier to climb into the ring and passively accept their thrashing.

Slocum hooked him again, and a terrified hush settled over the crowd.

No, this Slocum was no ordinary convict. Fighting him would be an entirely new experience. Herr Kaupfmann wiped his mouth with his black leather gloves, smearing them with his blood, and the salt sweat stung his cut lips.

El Comandante decided he liked the sensation.

Kaupfmann shuffled slowly toward Slocum, his head down. Slocum snapped his head back with another jab, then hooked his right eye one more time, closing it for good.

Kaupfmann moved back out of range and gave Slocum another ghastly grin. Slocum went after him. He stabbed him with another jab, another, then another. Again he hooked the bad eye, backed away, and then, moving in once more, he—

It was at this point that *Comandante* Kaupfmann kicked him in the right shin.

Slocum had been kicked before but never with a steel-toed high-top. He instantly lost all self-control. Raising his right leg, he grabbed the fractured shin and began hopping around the ring, his eyes burning with involuntary tears.

El Comandante grabbed him by the back of the head and butted him in the chin.

Slocum went down like a hammered steer.

When he came to, Jess had him on his stool. He was wiping his face off with a wet rag.

"You forgot to tell me he cheats," Slocum said.

"Usually, he doesn't have to."

Slocum was glaring at him again.

"Also keep an eye out on the referee."

"What?" Slocum was incredulous.

"You got to watch him like a hawk. Start to pull ahead, he'll disqualify you."

"So I can't win?"

"I didn't say that."

Jess unwound the blood stained bandages from Slocum's hands. He quietly slipped a thick four-inch rock spike into each of them, then quickly rewrapped the hands with fresh rags.

"I'm tellin' you," Jess said in his ear, "the key's the right side. Nail him there, then hook the head. He'll go down."

The bell rang, and the mob was screaming. Jess pulled Slocum to his feet, rubbing more neat's-foot oil on his nose and around his eyes, then pushed him back into the ring.

"Watch his boots," Jess screamed.

Slocum moved into the center of the ring. Okay, you sonofabitch, try this on for size. He feinted with the jab, then waited while Kaupfmann raised both his hands. When he lowered them, Slocum weighed in with a straight right, getting every ounce of his 220 pounds into the punch.

El Comandante lowered his head at the last second and caught the punch on the forehead.

Ordinarily, the blow would have broken every bone in Slocum's right hand, but tonight the rock spike turned his fist into an anvil. The shock shot straight up his arm and stung his shoulder.

To Slocum's horror, Kaupfmann shook it off and gave him another ghastly grin.

This was not the first time Slocum had seen such a grin. Warden Abner Hossett in Yuma Prison had decided it was his God-given duty to break Slocum and had personally supervised Slocum's floggings. Wrists lashed to the flogging post, the captain of the guard laying the bullwhip on with a will, Slocum could still see the warden's hellish grin, his voice audible above the blacksnake's crack:

"I'll break you yet, John Slocum. Bust you down to suckin' eggs. The man ain't been born Warden Abner Hossett can't break. You'll embrace your Maker 'fore I'm done with you. Embrace him on bended knee, cleansed in the Lamb's Own Blood."

That warden hadn't broken Slocum either.

But of course, he hadn't kicked him with steel-toed boots.

Again, Slocum waded in. Kaupfmann missed with a second kick, and when he tried to grab him for another butt, Slocum spun out of his sweat-slick grip, half gagging on the man's stink.

Kaupfmann's sweat smelled like urine.

Damn, his liver *must* be going.

Again, Slocum feinted to the *Comandante*'s face, and when Kaupfmann raised his hands, Slocum stomped on his right instep and hooked him under the right ribs as hard as he knew how.

Breath whooshed out of Kaupfmann with an awful rush, and he doubled over, clutching his side.

Slocum hooked him in the gut this time, as low as he could without fouling him. The *Comandante* started to double over a second time, so Slocum drove an uppercut straight under his chin and stomped on his other foot so hard the *Comandante*'s left instep cracked.

Kaupfmann was still upright, unable to fall with Slocum standing on his feet.

Slocum hit him again. For all he knew it was a lethal blow. Punching a man whose feet are pinned will usually crack the neck vertebrae. But Slocum didn't care.

He had to put him away.

Finally, he backed off the *Comandante*'s feet. The man was crumpling, but Slocum had to be sure. He spun sideways, then hammered the *Comandante*'s right side with the edge of his right fist.

Slocum had a half inch of rock spike bulging under the bandages, and he drove it straight into the *Comandante*'s liver.

Kaupfmann dropped to his hands and knees, spitting and gagging. He fought to get back up, but his elbows buckled, and he fell flat on his face, breaking his nose on the planking.

Rolling onto his side, his mouth foaming blood, he began to vomit.

Suddenly, Jess was in the ring beside Slocum, but instead of holding up his arm in victory, he shouted in his ear:

"Get the ref! Nail the bastard!"

He had to. The man was pointing at Slocum, and the neck whistle was in his mouth.

He was about to disqualify Slocum.

Slocum rushed him. Giving the ref a big winner's bear hug, he surreptitiously kneed him. The ref's legs gave way, and his mouth opened wide, gasping for air.

Slocum buried the ref's face in his chest so no one could see what he was about to do next: He jammed the whistle down the man's throat.

Then he dropped the ref on the floor beside Herr Kaupf-mann.

"Get to the hacienda pronto," Jess shouted to him.

Slocum quickly slipped away from the ring and headed for the main house.

Jess could deal with *El Comandante* and the gagging ref. After all, Jess had the next fight.

65

As Gokhlayeh walked along the top of the wall, the crowd below roared. He could not understand why. The fight had been violent. He would give the *pindah-lickoyee* that. Even now two men were choking and puking on their knees. But it was pointless violence.

Typical of the *pindah*s, he thought.

Well, maybe not all that pointless. The violence had drawn the sentries to this middle portion of the wall and distracted them. They still stared fixedly at the bizarre battle and ignored him as he passed.

Even now, he entered the gun tower unchallenged.

The Gatling gunner had his back to Geronimo. He, too, was yelling at the fighters below. "*Conchinos! Cabras! Hideputas!*" Pigs! Goats! Sons of whores! he shouted.

He glanced at Geronimo over his shoulder. "Ey, *amigo*, what are you doing here?"

"I'm your *relieve*." Relief.

"I no know you. It ain't time anyway. It ain't—Ey, no—Ey—"

Geronimo—approaching the guard from the back—grabbed his mouth, pulled back his head, and cut his throat. He jammed the corpse against the gun tower door.

Now there was nothing to do except wait for support.

216

Geronimo settled in behind the Gatling. He was nothing if not patient.

Almost as an afterthought he peered through the firing slit and watched the action in the ring below.

66

On the far side of the prison, Frank James, still in his *federale* uniform, made his way along the top of the wall. He was having difficulty spotting Doc. Looking across the yard, he finally saw him, on the hacienda roof. He was supposed to be lowering himself onto the fourth-story veranda on a rope. Instead he was doubled over coughing, his face buried in a bloodstained handkerchief.

Doc didn't look as if he would make it.

Frank wasn't all that sure about himself. An old Missouri croaker had once told him that he suffered from "a pathological fear of heights." He wasn't sure what *pathological* meant, but if it meant that your knees turned to chicken soup, your hands shook, and you couldn't stop gagging, he guessed he had it.

Even worse, the footing was bad. Adobe brick was hardly as durable as concrete, and these walls had been erected over a hundred years ago. Their tops were not only cracked and eroded, the edges had been beveled to begin with.

Frank was walking a thin and crumbly line.

He glanced at the opposite wall. It had the better view of the boxing match, so most of the sentries had crowded onto it.

Suddenly, he spotted Geronimo walking along its top.

He seemed to be having no trouble. The sentries were all drinking mescal and watching the boxing match below. The Apache was making good progress.

But enough of Geronimo. He had to watch his step—and to get to that gun tower.

He was making good time and was now within a hundred paces of the tower when his footing gave way.

The adobe crumbled beneath his feet like stale cake.

His limbs went weak, and he was overwhelmed by nausea.

His last thought was that he was about to die, and he was surprised to realize he didn't care.

He felt himself spinning wildly, erratically, out of control. He was falling, falling, falling. It seemed to take forever, and when, in the end, he did land, it was with a colossal jolt. Then the lights dimmed, faded, went out—and the world went black.

Frank James was sure he was dead.

After all, if this wasn't death, what else could it be?

Then Frank was sure of nothing, questioned nothing, wanted nothing.

Frank James knew nothing.

Frank was gone.

67

Doc Holliday halted on the hacienda's roof top and dropped to his knees.

He felt even worse than Frank.

For one thing his consumption was out of control, and every time he coughed it felt as if someone were taking a wood rasp to his lungs.

For another thing, his *federale* uniform—taken off the body of a dead sentry—was infested with crabs and lice. Every inch of his body seethed with vermin, and they were eating him alive.

If his body itched, his crotch was a field of fire.

He knew he was supposed to lower himself over the roof on a rope and onto Díaz's veranda. He knew he was supposed to be there when Slocum arrived, but he could not do it.

He could not even move.

He slipped the Henry rifle off his back and sat down on the rooftop. Doc was beaten. He knew that now.

He would die—all of them would—here or in La Fortaleza's mines.

Doc gave up. He had nothing left.

It took all his remaining strength to scratch his crotch.

68

John Slocum, phalanxed by a cadre of guards, reached the hacienda. While they hammered on the brass knocker, Slocum took a closer look at the old mansion. Five stories of spotlessly white adobe, it was surmounted by a slanting red-shingle roof. An imposing veranda, supported by massive white columns and corbels, dominated the facade.

A major let them in.

The front door opened directly into the *sala grande,* a spacious room filled with stained glass, heavy ceiling beams, polished oak floors, and pristine adobe walls, white-washed to a sparkling alabaster. The chairs were tall with high arms, upholstered in soft red leather and Andalusian velvet. Beside the chairs were round hand-carved tables. At the far end of the room was a fieldstone fireplace with shiny brass fire tools hanging in its massive maw.

A young sergeant of the guard directed Slocum toward a sweeping staircase of polished mahogany, which they followed to the fourth floor. On the way up the sergeant stroked his mustache and goatee. Finally he said under his breath:

"Ey, I got to hand it to you. You one lucky gringo, no?"

"You think so?"

"This is Díaz's *cuarto de dormir,*" his private chambers. "Inside are the most beautiful *putas* in all of Mejico. You

221

may die in the pits tomorrow, but tonight you live as a god.''

He said the word *god* with awe.

They reached Díaz's boudoir.

"The Gates of Paradise," the sergeant whispered.

The guard knocked three times. Two more uniformed guards opened the door and escorted him inside. They locked the others out.

The first thing Slocum heard was Don Porfirio's voice thundering through his drawing room.

"Señor Slocum, you were *magnífico!* I have never seen a better *pugilista.* You are indeed a *gachupin,*" a wearer of the spurs. "Tonight, *mi casa es su casa.* Everything I have is yours."

Slocum looked around. He was in a drawing room that opened up onto two adjoining boudoirs. He counted Díaz, four *soldados,* as well as Kate and Belle in full *puta* regalia.

To his dismay, Watley and Her Ladyship, garishly clad, entered from the veranda, grinning.

"As we say in the whorehouse," Watley said, "how's tricks?"

"Ask Captain Callahan."

While their laughter boomed, Slocum inspected the room more closely.

The main theme was military. The walls were covered with photos of *soldados* and *revolucionarios* in full uniforms, their chests crisscrossed with bandoliers, their faces haunted by shadowy sombreros, sweeping mustaches, and flat black eyes.

In the corner of the room, Slocum noted another nationality. *El Comandante* had hung photos of Prussian military cadets. These young men had blond hair, pale eyes, and their cheeks, like Kaupfmann's, were slashed by saber scars.

In between the photo collections were glass-encased dueling pistols, rifles, crossed sabers, and mounted animal heads—a bison, a puma, and an eight-point buck. On the floor were bearskin rugs.

Off to the side, a long table of polished teak was lavishly spread with ice buckets of champagne, wheels of Brie, strings of the *chorizo* sausage, platters of *frijoles*, *tortillas*, and *chiles* as well as *pan de campagne*.

Watley's laughter subsided. He and his friends were now seated on the teak settee and matching chair. They were imbibing Dom Perignon. They smiled at him pleasantly.

"And now," Her Ladyship said, "your *pièce de résistance*."

"The lovely Conchita," Watley said.

"The most beautiful *india virga* in all of Mejico," Díaz said.

She emerged from the near bedroom, attired in her white buckskins. Her raven hair was bundled vertically at the nape and wrapped in a *nah-leen*, or hair bow, in the style of Apache virgins.

"She is untouched by myself, by her own kind, or by *El Comandante*," Díaz said. "Tonight, she shall be yours alone."

Her black Apache eyes stared at Slocum, expressionless.

"Tonight," Díaz said, "you shall swim in champagne and dance with angels." He pronounced it "an-hels." "And you have earned it. *Madre Dios*, I have never seen such virtuosity. And to defeat *El Comandante*, no less? Whatever you desire, it shall be yours."

"I'd like to clean up."

"Come with me," Conchita said.

She led him to the *cuarto de baño*. It was furnished in white marble with brass fixtures. She poured a pitcher of hot water into a basin. He examined his face in the gilt-edged wall mirror behind it.

His eyes were swollen slits, and his smashed nostrils were caked with blood. His lips were split, and the rest of his face was covered with cuts and contusions.

After cleaning them up, he undressed and climbed into a hot steaming tub. Conchita slipped in behind him and began scrubbing his back.

"We must hurry," she said.

While he continued cleaning his cuts in a hand mirror, Díaz's voice roared in the other room:

"He is truly *muy macho, el supremo muy macho!*"

"Olé!" one of the guards shouted.

"You tell him," Belle said, getting into the spirit.

Kate let out with a "YIP-YIP-YIP-YIPPPINNNGGGG!" rebel yell.

Lady Hastings and His Lordship stared at them all with weary scorn.

"I say," Her Ladyship said, "doesn't *macho* have something to do with being a mu-u-ule?" She stretched the word into three derisive syllables.

"But of course," Díaz said.

He opened a bottle of 1811 Year-of-the-Comet Napoleon brandy, the most expensive cognac ever made.

"They are hardly as pretty as horses," Her Ladyship pointed out.

"But a true *hombre* cares nothing for pretty," Díaz said. "He maybe wants his *hijas*," his daughters, "pretty." The guards grinned. "He wants his flowers pretty." The guards nodded. "And, of course, he wants his *putas* pretty." The guards roared. "But for himself, he no cares for pretty. For himself he wants strength and power, endurance and *cojones*. A true *hombre* wants to be *muy macho*." Very mule-like.

"Hate to break it to you," Lady Hastings said, "but mule *cojones* are sterile."

"So much the better," Díaz said. "For *uno hombre macho* the *chingata*," the sex act, "is everything. The product, *nada*."

"Children mean nothing to him?" Watley asked.

"Less than nothing," Díaz said. "He leaves his bastards on his backtrail. With his whores."

"Mules are definitely good at that *chingata* stuff," Belle had to admit.

"*Naturalmente*," said Díaz. "They are *el supremo*. When a *macho* takes a mare, he has a *garrocha* like a *canon*, and he never quits. He is not like your horse who goes *bang!*"—Díaz clapped his hands—"and is finished. The *macho* will never let go. You cannot drive him off his *mujer*," his female partner, "with whips, prod poles, *pistolas*."

"You think Slocum is the same?" Lady Hastings asked.

"I always recognize the true *hombre duro*. It will be the same with Slocum and his *mujer*. It will be *stupendo!*"

"Your bath is over," Conchita whispered in Slocum's ear.

Slocum was still cleaning his battered face. "You think so?"

"I know so. Don Porfirio thinks you are *muy hombre*. You must not keep him waiting. One thing I have learned at La Fortaleza is you do not keep the Don waiting."

"You think I care?"

"I know you care, *pindah*. You care about your gold. You care about escape. And most of all, you care about your gun."

"You got me a gun?"

"It is hidden next to the bed."

John Slocum climbed out of the bath.

69

Jess lay facedown on the boxing platform. The guard, who was supposed to be his second, was laughing too hard to be of any help, and Jess himself was in serious agony. His arms and shoulders had taken so many punches, they were numb with pain and completely useless. He was having a hell of a time pushing himself up off the platform.

He finally rolled over and sat up. God, his stomach muscles ached. Too many shots to the old solar plexus as well.

He waited till his eyes focused. He was sorry they had. The first thing he saw was his Yaqui opponent. He saw his square *indio* face, brown as an old hide. He saw the wide, angular cheekbones, hard as cast iron, and the white grinning teeth.

Christ, the guy was a tiger. He could not only take a punch, he hit like a bull elephant.

This was Jess's fourteenth trip to the deck.

Still he had to continue. If the fight came to an end, the *prisioneros* went back to their cells, and there was nothing left to distract the guards.

They would spot his friends.

It was the Yaqui or the hell-mines.

Jess had to choose which.

He was having a hard time making up his mind.

70

Slocum and Conchita lay in Díaz big canopied bed. They were half under the red silk sheets, whispering make-believe love words, stalling for time.

Periodically the dictator looked into the room and leered.

"He isn't going to be happy," Conchita said, "until you act like a *macho*."

"Don't want to disappoint him, but I'm a man, not no mule."

"If we have to buy time, I will make love to you."

"I told you I ain't no *macho*." He touched her coiled hair. "And I ain't violatin' no hair-bow virgins."

"If we do not do *something*, he'll send you to the cells."
Slocum pretended to kiss her.

"Do not be afraid. I will be all right."

"You're Geronimo's woman."

She giggled at that one. "If he finds out you lay with me, even in innocence, he will skin you like a rabbit, then hang you by your feet over a slow-burning fire." She giggled again.

"Ey," Díaz roared, "how's my *macho?*"

"*Muy bueno*," Slocum yelled out. "She is one fine *puta*."

227

"The most beautiful *india pura* I have ever seen!" Díaz roared.

"Where's that gun you hid?" Slocum whispered.

"Near your waist between the bed and the wall. I had to gouge out part of the wall and force it in."

Slocum could feel part of the gun butt under the sheets. It was jammed into the wall *real* tight.

"I'll have to push back the bed to get it out," Slocum said.

"It had to be well hid."

"Ey, gringo," Díaz roared. "I told my friends you are *muy hombre*. What is happening, ey?" There was clear irritation in his voice.

"It does not do to keep his *Excelencia* waiting," La Conchita said.

She reached down with one hand and stroked the immensity of Slocum's manhood. With her other hand, she pulled him toward her.

"Show me the thing the *pindah*s call the ke-e-e-ss."

"I said I ain't violatin' no hair-bow virgins."

"Ey, gringo, I come in and show you how to do it myself," Díaz shouted. "You like that, no?"

She put her mouth on Slocum's, experimentally.

"Got it covered, *El Presidente*," Slocum yelled back.

Taking his hips in her hands, Conchita pulled Slocum onto her.

71

Bob Ford and the two stocky Chiricahuas silently pushed the handcart toward the wall. The cart—covered over with dirt and sagebrush—was filled with capped dynamite and ready to blow.

Finally they reached the wall. Ford flicked a lucifer with his thumb and, shielding it with his other hand, lit the sixty-second fuse.

"Ey, *amigo*," the sentry overhead yelled down at them, "what you doin'?"

They tore ass back to the nearby rocks, the man's shouts following them every step of the way.

"Ey, what's goin' on down there?"

Bob Ford hoped and prayed Slocum and the girls would have enough time.

72

Conchita's sobbing moans tore through the drawing room, rose to an ear-shattering pitch, peaked, crescendoed, then reverberated on and on and on through the hacienda.

Díaz was ecstatic. "He is indeed *muy hombre,* I can always tell. One *hombre macho* always knows another."

Someone began hammering on the door, and when the guard opened it, *El Comandante* limped in.

He looked terrible. His nose was broken and still bleeding, his right eye swollen shut, and he limped badly, clutching his right side.

He was greeted by another series of throat-rasping sobs, followed by gasping pleas.

"More! More! You are truly *muy macho!*" La Conchita cried out.

"Is this the one you called an Ice Queen?" Díaz asked *El Comandante.* "The one you were putting off because she was *mucha fría,*" too cold? "She sounds *mucha mujer,*" much woman, "to me."

Even Watley and Hastings had stopped sneering.

But *El Comandante* was not impressed. Pulling a pair of crossed sabers off the wall, he screamed:

"DI-I-R-R-R-R-R-R-N-E!" Whore!

And charged into the bedroom, sabers raised.

73

"DI-I-I-R-R-R-R-R-N-E!" filled the bedroom, and Slocum started pushing the bed away from the wall, clawing frantically at the gun.

It was stuck.

El Comandante towered above them, the military saber flashing overhead, beginning its downward sweep.

Conchita slipped a clasp knife out from under the mattress and, wheeling around, buried it, backhanded into *El Comandante*'s groin.

He dropped the sabers with a crash and collapsed onto the floor, fumbling at his crotch like a wounded bear.

The room swarmed with *soldados*.

Then, suddenly, they heard the noise. It started with a *ka-ka-ka,* which grew into *kaaaaaaaa,* which expanded into a *kaaaa-whummmmmp-kaaa-whummmmppp!* which climaxed in a shuddering, ear-cracking *KA!WHUMP! WHUMP!WHUMP!WHUMMMPPP!*

Slocum stared out the bedroom window.

A ball of smoke was rising above the far prison wall. Slowly it metamorphosed into fire. The ball grew bigger, bigger, bigger, till the top of the rising ball detonated with a thunderous *KU-WHUMPPP!*

Slowly the ball receded, fire and charred debris falling all over the prison yard.

When it dispersed, the wall was gone.

Suddenly, from the doorway, Slocum heard a friendly voice.

"Sorry I was late, John."

"You was born late, Doc."

When he turned around, Slocum saw that Belle and Kate had Díaz pressed up against the wall. Kate held a derringer pressed against his cheek. Belle kept a pepperbox to his balls.

"Give it up, *Presidente*," Belle said.

She cocked the hammer on the pepperbox.

"*Jamás!*" he snarled. Never. Turning to his men, he said: "Kill them all."

When Slocum took his hand from beside the bed, it was holding a .44 Remington.

When Doc levered his Henry, its *click-click!* filled the room.

Then he and Doc did what they did best.

They started killing people.

74

Jess lay facedown in the ring, covered with smoke-blackened debris. When he looked up, he saw that the prison wall, where the sentries had been standing, was gone.

He also saw an *indio*-looking *federale* with a Gatling gun wiping out the rest of the guards, as was a big, mean-looking gringo *federale* with a Spencer, posted behind a freight wagon.

Geronimo and Frank had come through.

All that was left was the big Yaqui in the ring, standing with his back to Jess, staring at the goings-on in awe.

Jess crawled to the edge of the platform. Reaching under the planking, his fists closed around the two rock spikes he'd given Slocum.

Turning around, he studied the back of the Yaqui's head.

75

From his position behind the freight wagon, Frank James's
Spencer commanded the entire yard. It wasn't as good as
a Gatling gun tower, but it was good enough. He'd nailed
one Gatling gunner dead-bang, and he was doing fine with
the guards.

For the most part they were armed with ancient muzzle-
loaders and handguns, and, lacking the powder for practice,
couldn't shoot worth beans.

Yes, for the first time all evening Frank was feeling good,
damn good. It actually looked like they would make it.

Then over by the cells he saw a guard strike a match.
Levering his Spencer, he shot the screw where he stood.

But could not stop what the man had done.

He could not stop the lighting of the fuse.

76

esse James nailed the back of the Yaqui's head as if he
were driving the last spike on the first transcontinental rail-
oad. The man fell so hard he bounced.

To Jesse's relief, he did not get back up.

Suddenly, he heard Frank alongside the ring. He had a
orse for him.

"Move it," Frank was yelling. "The damn place is going
o blow."

"Where's the others?"

"Ford's getting them."

Over by the hacienda, Bob Ford was holding a jerk line
f a half-dozen horses. Jess noted that Díaz, a man, and a
woman had their hands tied behind their backs and were
eing hoisted onto saddles.

"Let's went!" Frank yelled.

Jess jumped onto his mount and made tracks toward the
still-smoking wall.

77

Slocum and Conchita were a hundred yards past the prison when the cliff blew.

It made the destruction of the wall look a wet firecracker

The cliff face, housing nearly a thousand cells, turned into a massive sheet of flame. The ground trembled, and they could not control their mounts.

Still, Slocum—fighting both his reins and the jerk line—saw it all: fire pouring down on the prison, incinerating every building, scorching every inch of earth, engulfing La Fortaleza in a raging ocean of flames.

Silhouetted against the firestorm were two thousand escaping convicts, gushing out of the broken wall.

"What we gonna do with Díaz and the Limeys?" Slocum asked.

"What do you think?" Conchita said.

"Díaz starts braggin' on my *machismo* again, your man's gonna skin you alive."

"What do you think he'll do to *you?*"

For a long moment, they watched the spectacle. The fire continued to rain down, and the mob continued to roar through the prison wall—like the Wrath of God, like something out of hell itself. Ragged, filthy, starving, their lips were pulled back in wolfish snarls, and they were screaming for blood.

"I say we donate a little horse meat to the Cause," Slocum said.

"My people consider it a rare delicacy."

Slocum and Conchita trotted over to their three trussed-up hostages.

"Think you forgot somethin'," Slocum said.

"Now what could that be, sport?" Watley asked.

Conchita removed the quirt from Her Ladyship's tied-up wrist.

"The iron maiden in your *calabozo*," Conchita said. In your dungeon. "It is very pretty, no?"

"And real *macho*," Slocum said. "How can you stand to be without it?"

Conchita was already turning their mounts around.

"You really don't have to do this," Watley said.

"Quite all right," Her Ladyship protested.

"No bother at all," said Slocum.

Conchita cracked Her Ladyship's quirt across their horses' rumps. Hands tied behind backs, the trio galloped into the escaping mob.

The *prisioneros* folded over them like the sea.

"Hey, you two!" Jess called from behind. "Better catch up. If you still want your gold, that is."

For one second Slocum was tempted to shoot him.

The next second he laughed.

"What is so funny?" Conchita asked.

"It's hard to explain," Slocum said. "It's really hard."

She threw her hands up, shook her head, and mumbled something inaudible about "*Pindah-lickoyee.*"

They turned their mounts around and galloped into Jesse's dust.

Epilogue

I'll love you like the Good Book, John.
I'll never do you wrong.

—Belle Starr

I'll be beholden.

—Kate Elder

78

John Slocum came to. Everything was a blur, and his head felt as if the Southern Pacific had been using it for a rail spike.

Finally his vision cleared. He still wasn't sure where he was. From the looks of the brown adobe walls, the brown sheets, and the brown-skinned *puta* lying beside him, he was in a whorehouse.

Slowly, his memory returned.

They'd ridden with Geronimo the whole way back, sticking to the high lines, the owlhoot trail, only splitting up after they crossed the border. Slocum and Conchita had, at the end, shared one carefully concealed glance, Slocum wondering: "What if . . . ?" Conchita's eyes were flat, black, unreadable as the grave.

By nightfall Slocum and his friends had reached the town of Deadfall, Arizona. They'd planned one final blowout— tequila and cerveza, putas and pesos—before dividing the loot and going their separate ways.

As usual, the mejicano food had made his gut uneasy, and Belle had offered him another snort of her Lydia Pinkham's.

"Good for what ails you, John."

Then one final chaotic night of Belle and Kate—swarming

241

him like snakes, drowning him like the sea, consuming him like fire—leaving him burnt out, busted, dead.

When he came to, he'd had the worst hangover of his life, and the girls were gone.

In their place, on this bed, had lain two bags of dust— and two notes of farewell.

He'd opened the bags first.

There'd been gold in them—a couple of inches along the top.

The next dozen inches were ground pyrite—fool's gold.

Now, two weeks later—two weeks of drinking and whoring up the little gold dust they'd left him—he still trembled when he thought of the Jameses betrayal. And of those notes. The gall of those girls—the sheer vicious unmitigated gall. He could still see those notes before him—foul as a fart in church, plain as the balls on a tall dog.

I'll love you like the Good Book, John.
I'll never do you wrong.

—Belle Starr

I'll be beholden.
—Kate Elder

His hand still trembling, he reached for his bedside bottle. Damn it, the bottle was empty.

He considered smashing it against the wall, but something caught his eye. Strewn across the foot of the bed was a copy of the *Tombstone Epitaph.*

Somehow he'd missed the headline:

MISSOURI INCREASES BOUNTY ON JAMES BROTHERS!

Picking the paper up, Slocum looked at the article, confounded. The body copy read:

"Special Agent Allan Pinkerton has informed Governor Crittenden of Missouri that the nefarious James brothers have returned to Missouri. Crittenden says: 'Some of my political opponents have denounced me for increasing the bounty on these ruffians. They say I am a brutal man when I offer these Dead-Or-Alive rewards. They say my order to shoot them on sight is cruel and inhumane. I say these critics are weak-kneed bleeding hearts. The only way to rehabilitate nefarious scoundrels such as the James brothers is with a taut noose, the barrel of a gun, and dirt shoveled on their graves. I am therefore making it official. The State of Missouri is increasing the bounty on the Jameses: $55,000 for Jesse and $25,000 for his heinous brother, Frank.'

"Critics say that Crittenden is over-reacting to Jesse James's repeated threats to 'cut Crittenden's heart into strips and eat it whole.'

"Whatever the case, Frank and Jesse James are back in Missouri, and, once more, the chase is on."

The sun rose above the eastern rimrock, and light flooded Slocum's room. Reaching under his bed, he felt for his Winchester and Sharps.

They were still there.

"Eighty thousand dollars total, huh?" he said to the sleeping *puta*. "Just what they stoled from me."

She snorted hoarsely and pulled the pillow over her head.

Slocum got up. Slipping into his pants, he fumbled through his pockets until he found a double eagle. He squeezed it into the sleeping *puta*'s hand. Her fist closed over it like a vise.

Slocum pulled on his boots, hat, and his shirt.

Getting out his guns, he checked the loads.

It was time to get back to work, but not to the high lines, the owlhoot trail, not this time.

John Slocum was going to lend law and order a hand.

A special offer for people who enjoy reading the best Westerns published today. If you enjoyed this book, subscribe now and get...

TWO FREE WESTERNS!
A $5.90 VALUE—NO OBLIGATION

If you enjoyed this book and would like to read more of the very best Westerns being published today, you'll want to subscribe to True Value's Western Home Subscription Service. If you enjoyed the book you just read and want more of the most exciting, adventurous, action packed Westerns, subscribe now.

TWO FREE BOOKS

When you subscribe, we'll send you your first month's shipment of the newest and best 6 Westerns for you to preview. With your first shipment, two of these books will be yours as our introductory gift to you absolutely FREE, regardless of what you decide to do.

Special Subscriber Savings

As a True Value subscriber all regular monthly selections will be billed at the low subscriber price of just $2.45 each. That's at least a savings of $3.00 each month below the publishers price. There is never any shipping, handling or other hidden charges. What's more there is no minimum number of books you must buy, you may return any selection for full credit and you can cancel your subscription at any time. A TRUE VALUE!

Mail the coupon below

To start your subscription and receive 2 FREE WESTERNS, fill out the coupon below and mail it today. We'll send your first shipment which includes 2 FREE BOOKS as soon as we receive it.